Henry James

Henry James OM (15 April 1843 – 28 February 1916) was an American-British author regarded as a key transitional figure between literary realism and literary modernism, and is considered by many to be among the greatest novelists in the English language. He was the son of Henry James Sr. and the brother of renowned philosopher and psychologist William James and diarist Alice James.

He is best known for a number of novels dealing with the social and marital interplay between émigré Americans, English people, and continental Europeans. Examples of such novels include The Portrait of a Lady, The Ambassadors, and The Wings of the Dove. His later works were increasingly experimental. In describing the internal states of mind and social dynamics of his characters, James often made use of a style in which ambiguous or contradictory motives and impressions were overlaid or juxtaposed in the discussion of a character's psyche.(Source: Wikipedia)

Literary works:

Watch and Ward (1871)
Roderick Hudson (1875)
The American (1877)
The Europeans (1878)
Confidence (1879)
Washington Square (1880)
The Portrait of a Lady (1881)
The Bostonians (1886)
The Princess Casamassima (1886)
The Reverberator (1888)
The Tragic Muse (1890)
The Other House (1896)
The Spoils of Poynton (1897)
What Maisie Knew (1897)
The Awkward Age (1899)
The Sacred Fount (1901)

THE COLLECTED WORKS
OF
HENRY JAMES
VOL. 12 (OF 36)

THE PATH OF DUTY
FOUR MEETINGS

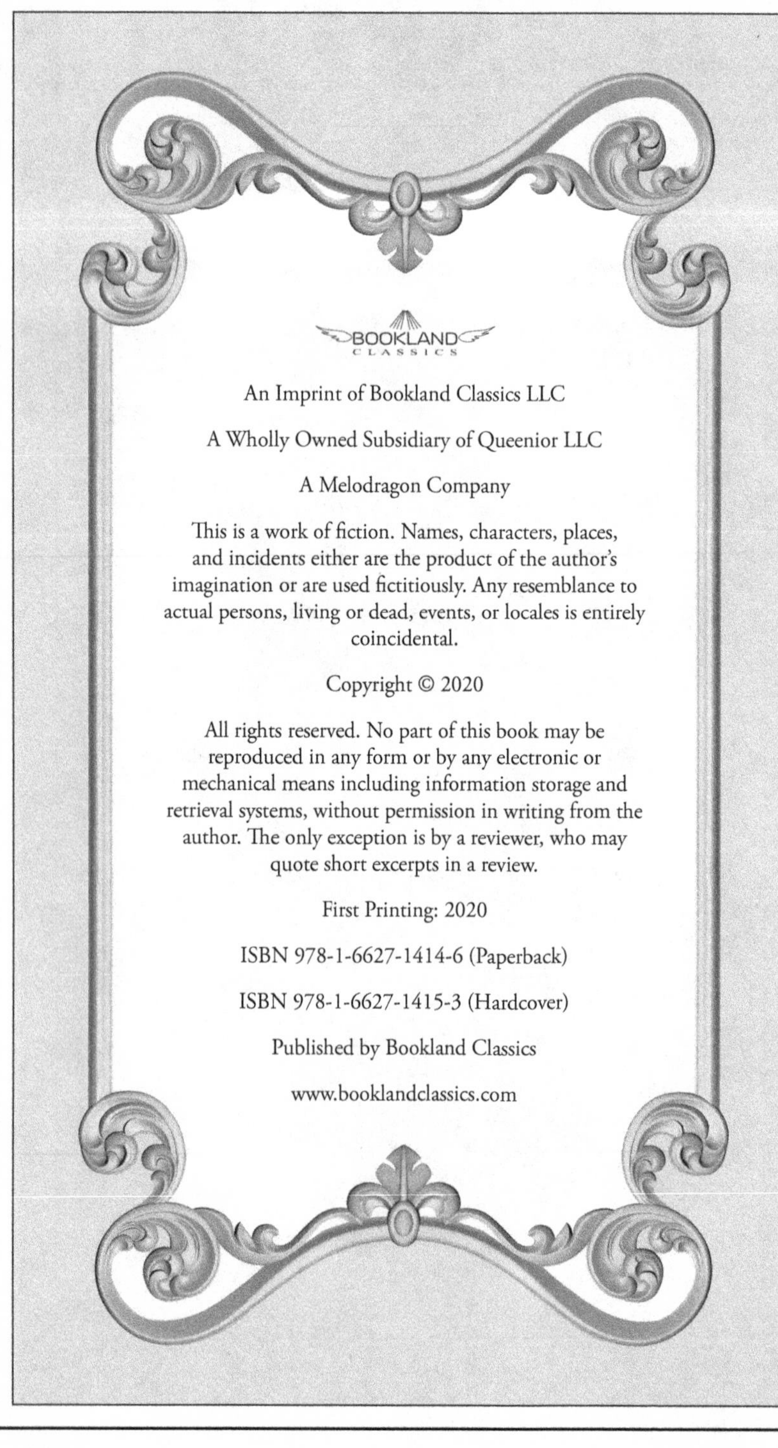

An Imprint of Bookland Classics LLC

A Wholly Owned Subsidiary of Queenior LLC

A Melodragon Company

This is a work of fiction. Names, characters, places, and incidents either are the product of the author's imagination or are used fictitiously. Any resemblance to actual persons, living or dead, events, or locales is entirely coincidental.

First Printing: 2020

ISBN 978-1-6627-1414-6 (Paperback)

ISBN 978-1-6627-1415-3 (Hardcover)

Published by Bookland Classics

www.booklandclassics.com

Contents

THE COLLECTED WORKS
OF
HENRY JAMES
VOL. 12 (OF 36)

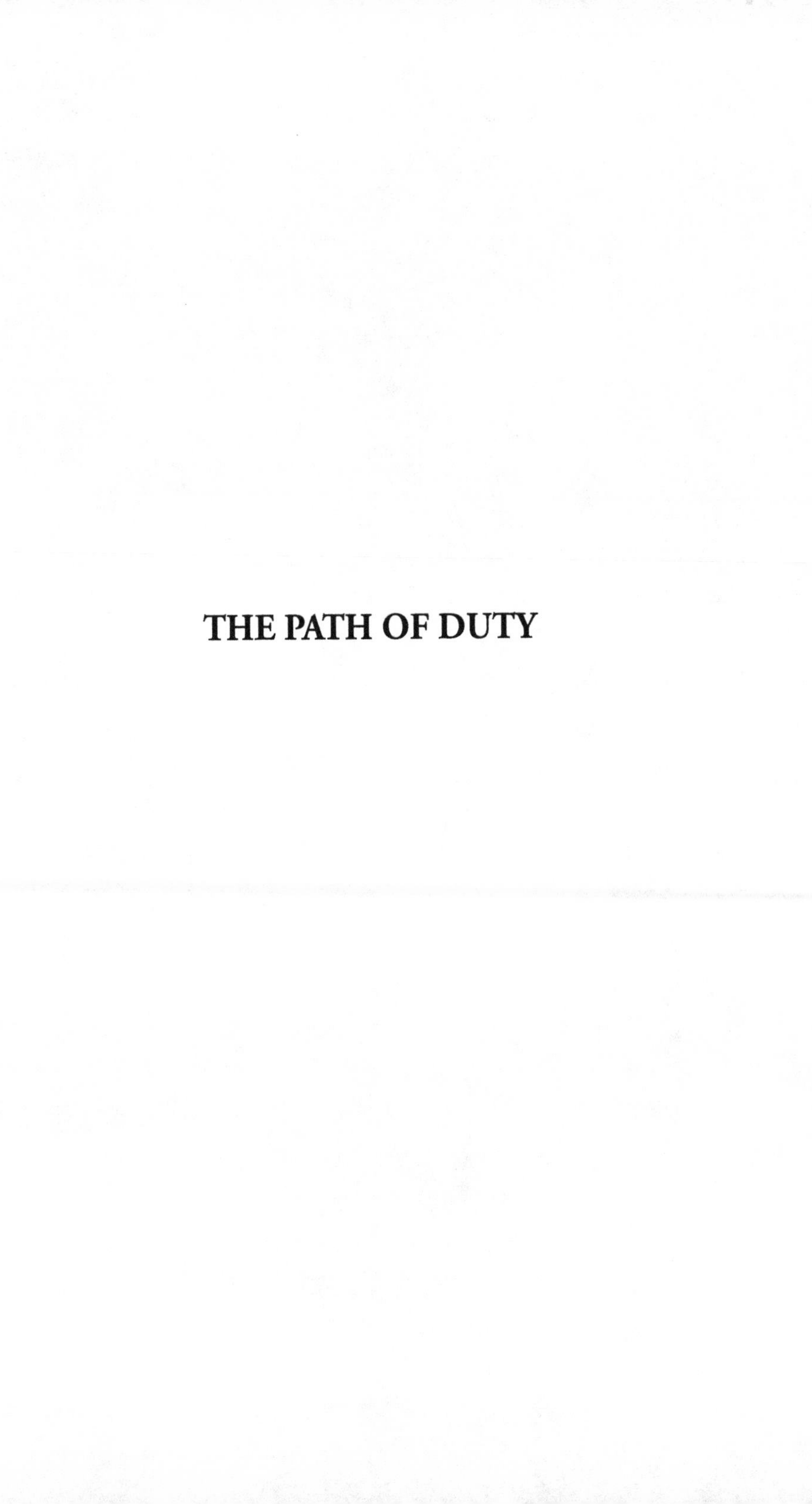

THE PATH OF DUTY

I am glad I said to you the other night at Doubleton, inquiring—too inquiring—compatriot, that I wouldn't undertake to tell you the story (about Ambrose Tester), but would write it out for you; inasmuch as, thinking it over since I came back to town, I see that it may really be made interesting. It *is* a story, with a regular development, and for telling it I have the advantage that I happened to know about it from the first, and was more or less in the confidence of every one concerned. Then it will amuse me to write it, and I shall do so as carefully and as cleverly as possible The first winter days in London are not madly gay, so that I have plenty of time; and if the fog is brown outside, the fire is red within. I like the quiet of this season; the glowing chimney-corner, in the midst of the December mirk, makes me think, as I sit by it, of all sorts of things. The idea that is almost always uppermost is the bigness and strangeness of this London world. Long as I have lived here,—the sixteenth anniversary of my marriage is only ten days off,—there is still a kind of novelty and excitement in it It is a great pull, as they say here, to have remained sensitive,—to have kept one's own point of view. I mean it's more entertaining,—it makes you see a thousand things (not that they are all very charming). But the pleasure of observation does not in the least depend on the beauty of what one observes. You see innumerable little dramas; in fact, almost everything has acts and scenes, like a comedy. Very often it is a comedy with tears. There have been a good many of them, I am afraid, in the case I am speaking of. It is because this history of Sir Ambrose Tester and Lady Vandeleur struck me, when you asked me about the relations of the parties, as having that kind of progression, that when I was on the point of responding, I checked myself, thinking it a pity to tell you a little when I might tell you all. I scarcely know what made you ask, inasmuch as I had said nothing to excite your curiosity. Whatever you suspected, you suspected on your own hook, as they say. You had simply noticed the pair together that evening at Doubleton. If you suspected anything in particular, it is a proof that you are rather sharp, because they are very careful about the way they behave in public. At least they think they are. The result, perhaps, doesn't necessarily follow. If I have been in their confidence you may say that I make a strange use of my privilege in serving them up to feed the prejudices of an opinionated American. You think English society very wicked, and my little story will probably not correct the impression. Though, after all, I don't see why it should minister to it; for what I said to you (it was all I did say) remains the truth. They are treading together the path of duty. You would be quite right about its being base in me to betray them. It is very true that they have ceased to confide in me; even Joscelind has said nothing to me for more than a year. That is doubtless a sign that the situation is more serious than before, all round,—too serious to be talked about. It is also true that you are remarkably discreet, and that even if you were not it would not make much difference, inasmuch as if you were to repeat my revelations in America, no one would know whom you were talking about. But all the same, I should be base; and, therefore, after I have written out my reminiscences for your delectation, I shall simply keep them for my own. You must content yourself with the explanation I have already given you of Sir Ambrose Tester and Lady Vandeleur: they are following—hand in hand, as it were—the path of duty. This will not prevent me from telling everything; on the contrary, don't you see?

I.

His brilliant prospects dated from the death of his brother, who had no children, had indeed steadily refused to marry. When I say brilliant prospects, I mean the vision of the baronetcy, one of the oldest in England, of a charming seventeenth-century house, with its park, in Dorsetshire, and a property worth some twenty thousand a year. Such a collection of items is still dazzling to me, even after what you would call, I suppose, a familiarity with British grandeur. My husband is n't a baronet (or we probably should n't be in London in December), and he is far, alas, from having twenty thousand a year. The full enjoyment of these luxuries, on Ambrose Tester's part, was dependent naturally, on the death of his father, who was still very much to the fore at the time I first knew the young man. The proof of it is the way he kept nagging at his sons, as the younger used to say, on the question of taking a wife. The nagging had been of no avail, as I have mentioned, with regard to Francis, the elder, whose affections were centred (his brother himself told me) on the winecup and the faro-table. He was not an exemplary or edifying character, and as the heir to an honorable name and a fine estate was very unsatisfactory indeed. It had been possible in those days to put him into the army, but it was not possible to keep him there; and he was still a very young man when it became plain that any parental dream of a "career" for Frank Tester was exceedingly vain. Old Sir Edmund had thought matrimony would perhaps correct him, but a sterner process than this was needed, and it came to him one day at Monaco—he was most of the time abroad—after an illness so short that none of the family arrived in time. He was reformed altogether, he was utterly abolished.

The second son, stepping into his shoes, was such an improvement that it was impossible there should be much simulation of mourning. You have seen him, you know what he is; there is very little mystery about him. As I am not going to show this composition to you, there is no harm in my writing here that he is—or at any rate he was—a remarkably attractive man. I don't say this because he made love to me, but precisely because he did n't. He was always in love with some one else,—generally with Lady Vandeleur. You may say that in England that usually does n't prevent; but Mr. Tester, though he had almost no intermissions, did n't, as a general thing, have duplicates. He was not provided with a second loved object, "under-studying," as they say, the part. It was his practice to keep me accurately informed of the state of his affections,—a matter about which he was never in the least vague. When he was in love he knew it and rejoiced in it, and when by a miracle he was not he greatly regretted it. He expatiated to me on the charms of other persons, and this interested me much more than if he had attempted to direct the conversation to my own, as regards which I had no illusions. He has told me some singular things, and I think I may say that for a considerable period my most valued knowledge of English society was extracted from this genial youth. I suppose he usually found me a woman of good counsel, for certain it is that he has appealed to me for the light of wisdom in very extraordinary predicaments. In his earlier years he was perpetually in hot water; he tumbled into scrapes as children tumble into puddles. He invited them, he invented them; and when he came to tell you how his trouble had come about (and he always told the whole truth), it was difficult to believe that a man should have been so idiotic.

And yet he was not an idiot; he was supposed to be very clever, and certainly is very quick and amusing. He was only reckless, and extraordinarily natural, as natural as if he had been an Irishman. In fact, of all the Englishmen that I have known he is the most Irish in temperament (though he has got over it comparatively of late). I used to tell him that it was a great inconvenience that he didn't speak with a brogue, because then we should be forewarned, and know with whom we were dealing. He replied that, by analogy, if he were Irish enough to have a brogue he would probably be English, which seemed to me an answer wonderfully in character. Like most young Britons of his class he went to America, to see the great country, before he was twenty, and he took a letter to my father, who had occasion, *à propos* of some pickle of course, to render him a considerable service. This led to his coming to see me—I had already been living here three or four years—on his return; and that, in the course of time, led to our becoming fast friends, without, as I tell you, the smallest philandering on either side. But I must n't protest too much;

I shall excite your suspicion. "If he has made love to so many women, why should n't he have made love to you?"—some inquiry of that sort you will be likely to make. I have answered it already, "Simply on account of those very engagements." He could n't make love to every one, and with me it would n't have done him the least good. It was a more amiable weakness than his brother's, and he has always behaved very well. How well he behaved on a very important occasion is precisely the subject of my story.

He was supposed to have embraced the diplomatic career; had been secretary of legation at some German capital; but after his brother's death he came home and looked out for a seat in Parliament. He found it with no great trouble and has kept it ever since. No one would have the heart to turn him out, he is so good-looking. It's a great thing to be represented by one of the handsomest men in England, it creates such a favorable association of ideas. Any one would be amazed to discover that the borough he sits for, and the name of which I am always forgetting, is not a very pretty place. I have never seen it, and have no idea that it is n't, and I am sure he will survive every revolution. The people must feel that if they should n't keep him some monster would be returned. You remember his appearance,—how tall, and fair, and strong he is, and always laughing, yet without looking silly. He is exactly the young man girls in America figure to themselves—in the place of the hero—when they read English novels, and wish to imagine something very aristocratic and Saxon. A "bright Bostonian" who met him once at my house, exclaimed as soon as he had gone out of the room, "At last, at last, I behold it, the mustache of Roland Tremayne!"

"Of Roland Tremayne!"

"Don't you remember in *A Lawless Love*, how often it's mentioned, and how glorious and golden it was? Well, I have never seen it till now, but now I *have* seen it!"

If you had n't seen Ambrose Tester, the best description I could give of him would be to say that he looked like Roland Tremayne. I don't know whether that hero was a "strong Liberal," but this is what Sir Ambrose is supposed to be. (He succeeded his father two years ago, but I shall come to that.) He is not exactly what I should call thoughtful, but he is interested, or thinks he is, in a lot of things that I don't understand, and that one sees and skips in the newspapers,—volunteering, and redistribution, and sanitation, and the representation of minors—minorities—what is it? When I said just now that he is always laughing, I ought to have explained that I did n't mean when he is talking to Lady Vandeleur. She makes him serious, makes him almost solemn; by which I don't mean that she bores him. Far from it; but when he is in her company he is thoughtful; he pulls his golden mustache, and Roland Tremayne looks as if his vision were turned in, and he were meditating on her words. He does n't say much himself; it is she—she used to be so silent—who does the talking. She has plenty to say to him; she describes to him the charms that she discovers in the path of duty. He seldom speaks in the House, I believe, but when he does it's offhand, and amusing, and sensible, and every one likes it. He will never be a great statesman, but he will add to the softness of Dorsetshire, and remain, in short, a very gallant, pleasant, prosperous, typical English gentleman, with a name, a fortune, a perfect appearance, a devoted, bewildered little wife, a great many reminiscences, a great many friends (including Lady Vandeleur and myself), and, strange to say, with all these advantages, something that faintly resembles a conscience.

II.

Five years ago he told me his father insisted on his marrying,—would not hear of his putting it off any longer. Sir Edmund had been harping on this string ever since he came back from Germany, had made it both a general and a particular request, not only urging him to matrimony in the abstract, but pushing him into the arms of every young woman in the country. Ambrose had promised, procrastinated, temporized; but at last he was at the end of his evasions, and his poor father had taken the tone of supplication. "He thinks immensely of the name, of the place and all that, and he has got it into his head that if I don't marry before he dies, I won't marry after." So much I remember Ambrose Tester said to me. "It's a fixed idea; he has got it on the brain. He wants to see me married with his eyes, and he wants to take his grandson in his arms. Not without that will he be satisfied that the whole thing will go straight. He thinks he is nearing his end, but he isn't,—he will live to see a hundred, don't you think so?—and he has made me a solemn appeal to put an end to what he calls his suspense. He has an idea some one will get hold of me—some woman I can't marry. As if I were not old enough to take care of myself!"

"Perhaps he is afraid of me," I suggested, facetiously.

"No, it is n't you," said my visitor, betraying by his tone that it was some one, though he didn't say whom. "That's all rot, of course; one marries sooner or later, and I shall do like every one else. If I marry before I die, it's as good as if I marry before he dies, is n't it? I should be delighted to have the governor at my wedding, but it is n't necessary for the legality, is it?"

I asked him what he wished me to do, and how I could help him. He knew already my peculiar views, that I was trying to get husbands for all the girls of my acquaintance and to prevent the men from taking wives. The sight of an ummarried woman afflicted me, and yet when my male friends changed their state I took it as a personal offence. He let me know that so far as he was concerned I must prepare myself for this injury, for he had given his father his word that another twelvemonth should not see him a bachelor. The old man had given him *carte blanche*; he made no condition beyond exacting that the lady should have youth and health. Ambrose Tester, at any rate, had taken a vow and now he was going seriously to look about him. I said to him that what must be must be, and that there were plenty of charming girls about the land, among whom he could suit himself easily enough. There was no better match in England, I said, and he would only have to make his choice. That however is not what I thought, for my real reflections were summed up in the silent exclamation, "What a pity Lady Vandeleur isn't a widow!" I hadn't the smallest doubt that if she were he would marry her on the spot; and after he had gone I wondered considerably what *she* thought of this turn in his affairs. If it was disappointing to me, how little it must be to *her* taste! Sir Edmund had not been so much out of the way in fearing there might be obstacles to his son's taking the step he desired. Margaret Vandeleur was an obstacle. I knew it as well as if Mr. Tester had told me.

I don't mean there was anything in their relation he might not freely have alluded to, for Lady Vandeleur, in spite of her beauty and her tiresome husband, was not a woman who could be accused of an indiscretion. Her husband was a pedant about trifles,—the shape of his hatbrim, the *pose* of his coachman, and cared for nothing else; but she was as nearly a saint as one may be when one has rubbed shoulders for ten years with the best society in Europe. It is a characteristic of that society that even its saints are suspected, and I go too far in saying that little pinpricks were not administered, in considerable numbers to her reputation. But she did n't feel them, for still more than Ambrose Tester she was a person to whose happiness a good conscience was necessary. I should almost say that for her happiness it was sufficient, and, at any rate, it was only those who didn't know her that pretended to speak of her lightly. If one had the honor of her acquaintance one might have thought her rather shut up to her beauty and her grandeur, but one could n't but feel there was something in her composition that would keep her from vulgar aberrations. Her husband was such a feeble type that she must have felt doubly she had been put upon her honor. To deceive such a man as that was to make him more ridiculous than he was already, and from such a result a woman bearing his name may very well have shrunk. Perhaps it would have been worse for Lord Vandeleur, who had every pretension of his order and none of its amiability, if he had been a better, or at least, a cleverer man. When a woman behaves so well she is not obliged to be careful, and there is no need of consulting appearances when one is one's self an appearance. Lady Vandeleur accepted Ambrose Tester's attentions, and Heaven knows they were frequent; but she had such an air of perfect equilibrium that one could n't see her, in imagination, bend responsive. Incense was incense, but one saw her sitting quite serene among the fumes. That honor of her acquaintance of which I just now spoke it had been given me to enjoy; that is to say, I met her a dozen times in the season in a hot crowd, and we smiled sweetly and murmured a vague question or two, without hearing, or even trying to hear, each other's answer. If I knew that Ambrose Tester was perpetually in and out of her house and always arranging with her that they should go to the same places, I doubt whether she, on her side, knew how often he came to see me. I don't think he would have let her know, and am conscious, in saying this, that it indicated an advanced state of intimacy (with her, I mean).

I also doubt very much whether he asked her to look about, on his behalf, for a future Lady Tester. This request he was so good as to make of me; but I told him I would have nothing to do with the matter. If Joscelind is unhappy, I am thankful to say the responsibility is not mine. I have found English husbands for two or three American girls, but providing English wives is a different affair. I know the sort of men that will suit women, but one would have to be very clever to know the sort of women that will suit men. I told Ambrose Tester that he must look out for himself, but, in spite of his promise, I had very little belief that he would do anything of the sort. I thought it probable that the old baronet would pass away without seeing a new generation come in; though when I intimated as much to Mr. Tester, he made answer in substance (it was not quite so crudely said) that his father, old as he was, would hold on till his bidding was done, and if it should not be done, he would hold on out of spite. "Oh, he will tire me out;" that I remember Ambrose Tester did say. I had done him injustice, for six months later he told me he was engaged. It had all come about very suddenly. From one day to the other the right young woman had been found. I forget who had found her; some aunt or cousin, I think; it had not been the young man himself. But when she was found, he rose to the occasion; he took her up seriously, he approved of her thoroughly, and I am not sure that he didn't fall a little in love with her, ridiculous (excuse my London tone) as this accident may appear. He told me that his father was delighted, and I knew afterwards that he had good reason to be. It was not till some weeks later that I saw the girl; but meanwhile I had received the pleasantest impression of her, and this impression came—must have come—mainly from what her intended told me. That proves that he spoke with some positiveness, spoke as if he really believed he was doing a good thing. I had it on my tongue's end to ask him how Lady Vandeleur liked her, but I fortunately checked this vulgar inquiry. He liked her evidently, as I say; every one liked her, and when I knew her I liked her better even than the others. I like her to-day more than ever; it is fair you should know that, in reading this account of her situation. It doubtless colors my picture, gives a point to my sense of the strangeness of my little story.

Joscelind Bernardstone came of a military race, and had been brought up in camps,—by which I don't mean she was one of those objectionable young women who are known as garrison hacks. She was in the flower of her freshness, and had been kept in the tent, receiving, as an only daughter, the most "particular" education from the excellent Lady Emily (General Bernardstone married a daughter of Lord Clandufly), who looks like a pink-faced rabbit, and is (after Joscelind) one of the nicest women I know. When I met them in a country-house, a few weeks after the marriage was "arranged," as they say here, Joscelind won my affections by saying to me, with her timid directness (the speech made me feel sixty years old), that she must thank me for having been so kind to Mr. Tester. You saw her at Doubleton, and you will remember that though she has no regular beauty, many a prettier woman would be very glad to look like her. She is as fresh as a new-laid egg, as light as a feather, as strong as a mail-phaeton. She is perfectly mild, yet she is clever enough to be sharp if she would. I don't know that clever women are necessarily thought ill-natured, but it is usually taken for granted that amiable women are very limited. Lady Tester is a refutation of the theory, which must have been invented by a vixenish woman who was *not* clever. She has an adoration for her husband, which absorbs her without in the least making her silly, unless indeed it is silly to be modest, as in this brutal world I sometimes believe. Her modesty is so great that being unhappy has hitherto presented itself to her as a form of egotism,—that egotism which she has too much delicacy to cultivate. She is by no means sure that if being married to her beautiful baronet is not the ideal state she dreamed it, the weak point of the affair is not simply in her own presumption. It does n't express her condition, at present, to say that she is unhappy or disappointed, or that she has a sense of injury. All this is latent; meanwhile, what is obvious, is that she is bewildered,—she simply does n't understand; and her perplexity, to me, is unspeakably touching. She looks about her for some explanation, some light. She fixes her eyes on mine sometimes, and on those of other people, with a kind of searching dumbness, as if there were some chance that I—that they—may explain, may tell her what it is that has happened to her. I can explain very well, but not to her,—only to you!

III.

It was a brilliant match for Miss Bernardstone, who had no fortune at all, and all her friends were of the opinion that she had done very well After Easter she was in London with her people, and I saw a good deal of them, in fact, I rather cultivated them. They might perhaps even have thought me a little patronizing, if they had been given to thinking that sort of thing. But they were not; that is not in their line. English people are very apt to attribute motives,—some of them attribute much worse ones than we poor simpletons in America recognize, than we have even heard of! But that is only some of them; others don't, but take everything literally and genially. That was the case with the Bernardstones; you could be sure that on their way home, after dining with you, they would n't ask each other how in the world any one could call you pretty, or say that many people *did* believe, all the same, that you had poisoned your grandfather.

Lady Emily was exceedingly gratified at her daughter's engagement; of course she was very quiet about it, she did n't clap her hands or drag in Mr. Tester's name; but it was easy to see that she felt a kind of maternal peace, an abiding satisfaction. The young man behaved as well as possible, was constantly seen with Joscelind, and smiled down at her in the kindest, most protecting way. They looked beautiful together; you would have said it was a duty for people whose color matched so well to marry. Of course he was immensely taken up, and did n't come very often to see me; but he came sometimes, and when he sat there he had a look which I did n't understand at first. Presently I saw what it expressed; in my drawing-room he was off duty, he had no longer to sit up and play a part; he would lean back and rest and draw a long breath, and forget that the day of his execution was fixed. There was to be no indecent haste about the marriage; it was not to take place till after the session, at the end of August It puzzled me and rather distressed me. that his heart should n't be a little more in the matter; it seemed strange to be engaged to so charming a girl and yet go through with it as if it were simply a social duty. If one had n't been in love with her at first, one ought to have been at the end of a week or two. If Ambrose Tester was not (and to me he did n't pretend to be), he carried it off, as I have said, better than I should have expected. He was a gentleman, and he behaved like a gentleman, with the added punctilio, I think, of being sorry for his betrothed. But it was difficult to see what, in the long run, he could expect to make of such a position. If a man marries an ugly, unattractive woman for reasons of state, the thing is comparatively simple; it is understood between them, and he need have no remorse at not offering her a sentiment of which there has been no question. But when he picks out a charming creature to gratify his father and *les convenances*, it is not so easy to be happy in not being able to care for her. It seemed to me that it would have been much better for Ambrose Tester to bestow himself upon a girl who might have given him an excuse for tepidity. His wife should have been healthy but stupid, prolific but morose. Did he expect to continue not to be in love with Joscelind, or to conceal from her the mechanical nature of his attentions? It was difficult to see how he could wish to do the one or succeed in doing the other. Did he expect such a girl as that would be happy if he did n't love her? and did he think himself capable of being happy if it should turn out that she was miserable? If she should n't be miserable,—that is, if she should be indifferent, and, as they say, console herself, would he like that any better?

I asked myself all these questions and I should have liked to ask them of Mr. Tester; but I did n't, for after all he could n't have answered them. Poor young man! he did n't pry into things as I do; he was not analytic, like us Americans, as they say in reviews. He thought he was behaving remarkably well, and so he was—for a man; that was the strange part of it. It had been proper that in spite of his reluctance he should take a wife, and he had dutifully set about it. As a good thing is better for being well done, he had taken the best one he could possibly find. He was enchanted with—with his young lady, you might ask? Not in the least; with himself; that is the sort of person a man is! Their virtues are more dangerous than their vices, and Heaven preserve you when they want to keep a promise! It is never a promise to *you*, you will notice. A man will sacrifice a woman to live as a gentleman should, and then ask for your sympathy—for *him*! And I don't speak of the bad ones, but of the good. They, after all, are the worst Ambrose Tester, as I say, did n't go into these details, but synthetic as he might be, was conscious that his position was false. He felt that sooner or later, and rather sooner than later, he would have to make it true,—a process that could n't possibly be agreeable. He would really have to make up his mind to care for his wife or not to care for her. What would Lady Vandeleur say to one alternative, and what would little Joscelind say to the other? That is what it was to have a pertinacious father and to be an accommodating son. With me, it was easy for Ambrose Tester to be superficial, for, as I tell you, if I did n't wish to engage him, I did n't wish to disengage him, and I did n't insist Lady Vandeleur insisted, I was afraid; to be with her was of course very complicated; even more than Miss Bernardstone she must have made him feel that his position was false. I must add that he once mentioned to me that she had told him he ought to marry. At any rate, it is an immense thing to be a pleasant fellow. Our young fellow was so universally pleasant that of course his *fiancée* came in for her share. So did Lady Emily, suffused with hope, which made her pinker than ever; she told me he sent flowers even to her. One day in the Park, I was riding early; the Row was almost empty. I came up behind a lady and gentleman who were walking their horses, close to each other, side by side In a moment I recognized her, but not before seeing that nothing could have been more benevolent than the way Ambrose Tester was bending over his future wife. If he struck me as a lover at that moment, of course he struck her so. But that is n't the way they ride to-day.

IV.

One day, about the end of June, he came in to see me when I had two or three other visitors; you know that even at that season I am almost always at home from six to seven. He had not been three minutes in the room before I saw that he was different,—different from what he had been the last time, and I guessed that something had happened in relation to his marriage. My visitors did n't, unfortunately, and they stayed and stayed until I was afraid he would have to go away without telling me what, I was sure, he had come for. But he sat them out; I think that by exception they did n't find him pleasant. After we were alone he abused them a little, and then he said, "Have you heard about Vandeleur? He 's very ill. She's awfully anxious." I had n't heard, and I told him so, asking a question or two; then my inquiries ceased, my breath almost failed me, for I had become aware of something very strange. The way he looked at me when he told me his news was a full confession,—a confession so full that I had needed a moment to take it in. He was not too strong a man to be taken by surprise,—not so strong but that in the presence of an unexpected occasion his first movement was to look about for a little help. I venture to call it help, the sort of thing he came to me for on that summer afternoon. It is always help when a woman who is not an idiot lets an embarrassed man take up her time. If he too is not an idiot, that does n't diminish the service; on the contrary his superiority to the average helps him to profit. Ambrose Tester had said to me more than once, in the past, that he was capable of telling me things, because I was an American, that he would n't confide to his own people. He had proved it before this, as I have hinted, and I must say that being an American, with him, was sometimes a questionable honor. I don't know whether he thinks us more discreet and more sympathetic (if he keeps up the system: he has abandoned it with me), or only more insensible, more proof against shocks; but it is certain that, like some other Englishmen I have known, he has appeared, in delicate cases, to think I would take a comprehensive view. When I have inquired into the grounds of this discrimination in our favor, he has contented himself with saying, in the British-cursory manner, "Oh, I don't know; you are different!" I remember he remarked once that our impressions were fresher. And I am sure that now it was because of my nationality, in addition to other merits, that he treated me to the confession I have just alluded to. At least I don't suppose he would have gone about saying to people in general, "Her husband will probably die, you know; then why should n't I marry Lady Vandeleur?"

That was the question which his whole expression and manner asked of me, and of which, after a moment, I decided to take no notice. Why shouldn't he? There was an excellent reason why he should n't It would just kill Joscelind Bernardstone; that was why he should n't? The idea that he should be ready to do it frightened me, and independent as he might think my point of view, I had no desire to discuss such abominations. It struck me as an abomination at this very first moment, and I have never wavered in my judgment of it. I am always glad when I can take the measure of a thing as soon as I see it; it 's a blessing to *feel* what we think, without balancing and comparing. It's a great rest, too, and a great luxury. That, as I say, was the case with the feeling excited in me by this happy idea of Ambrose Tester's. Cruel and wanton I thought it then, cruel and wanton I thought it later, when it was pressed upon me. I knew there were many other people that did n't agree with me, and I can only hope for them that their conviction was as quick and positive as mine; it all depends upon the way a thing strikes one. But I will add to this another remark. I thought I was right then, and I still think I was right; but it strikes me as a pity that I should have wished so much to be right Why could n't I be content to be wrong; to renounce my influence (since I appeared to possess the mystic article), and let my young friend do as he liked? As you observed the situation at Doubleton, should n't you say it was of a nature to make one wonder whether, after all, one did render a service to the younger lady?

At all events, as I say, I gave no sign to Ambrose Tester that I understood him, that I guessed what he wished to come to. He got no satisfaction out of me that day; it is very true that he made up for it later. I expressed regret at Lord Vandeleur's illness, inquired into its nature and origin, hoped it would n't prove as grave as might be feared, said I would call at the house and ask about him, commiserated discreetly her ladyship, and in short gave my young man no chance whatever. He knew that I had guessed his *arrière-pensée*, but he let me off for the moment, for which I was thankful; either because he was still ashamed of it, or because he supposed I was reserving myself for the catastrophe,—should it occur. Well, my dear, it did occur, at the end of ten days. Mr. Tester came to see me twice in that interval, each time to tell me that poor Vandeleur was worse; he had some internal inflammation which, in nine cases out of ten, is fatal. His wife was all devotion; she was with him night and day. I had the news from other sources as well; I leave you to imagine whether in London, at the height of the season, such a situation could fail to be considerably discussed. To the discussion as yet, however, I contributed little, and with Ambrose Tester nothing at all. I was still on my guard. I never admitted for a moment that it was possible there should be any change in his plans. By this time, I think, he had quite ceased to be ashamed of his idea, he was in a state almost of exaltation about it; but he was very angry with me for not giving him an opening.

As I look back upon the matter now, there is something almost amusing in the way we watched each other,—he thinking that I evaded his question only to torment him (he believed me, or pretended to believe me, capable of this sort of perversity), and I determined not to lose ground by betraying an insight into his state of mind which he might twist into an expression of sympathy. I wished to leave my sympathy where I had placed it, with Lady Emily and her daughter, of whom I continued, bumping against them at parties, to have some observation. They gave no signal of alarm; of course it would have been premature. The girl, I am sure, had no idea of the existence of a rival. How they had kept her in the dark I don't know; but it was easy to see she was too much in love to suspect or to criticise. With Lady Emily it was different; she was a woman of charity, but she touched the world at too many points not to feel its vibrations. However, the dear little woman planted herself firmly; to the eye she was still enough. It was not from Ambrose Tester that I first heard of Lord Vandeleur's death; it was announced, with a quarter of a column of "padding," in the *Times*. I have always known the *Times* was a wonderful journal, but this never came home to me so much as when it produced a quarter of a column about Lord Vandeleur. It was a triumph of word-spinning. If he had carried out his vocation, if he had been a tailor or a hatter (that's how I see him), there might have been something to say about him. But he missed his vocation, he missed everything but posthumous honors. I was so sure Ambrose Tester would come in that afternoon, and so sure he knew I should expect him, that I threw over an engagement on purpose. But he didn't come in, nor the next day, nor the next. There were two possible explanations of his absence. One was that he was giving all his time to consoling Lady Vandeleur; the other was that he was giving it all, as a blind, to Joscelind Bernardstone. Both proved incorrect, for when he at last turned up he told me he had been for a week in the country, at his father's. Sir Edmund also had been unwell; but he had pulled through better than poor Lord Vandeleur. I wondered at first whether his son had been talking over with him the question of a change of base; but guessed in a moment that he had not suffered this alarm. I don't think that Ambrose would have spared him if he had thought it necessary to give him warning; but he probably held that his father would have no ground for complaint so long as he should marry some one; would have no right to remonstrate if he simply transferred his contract. Lady Vandeleur had had two children (whom she had lost), and might, therefore, have others whom she should n't lose; that would have been a reply to nice discriminations on Sir Edmund's part.

V.

In reality, what the young man had been doing was thinking it over beneath his ancestral oaks and beeches. His countenance showed this,—showed it more than Miss Bernardstone could have liked. He looked like a man who was crossed, not like a man who was happy, in love. I was no more disposed than before to help him out with his plot, but at the end of ten minutes we were articulately discussing it. When I say *we* were, I mean he was; for I sat before him quite mute, at first, and amazed at the clearness with which, before his conscience, he had argued his case. He had persuaded himself that it was quite a simple matter to throw over poor Joscelind and keep himself free for the expiration of Lady Vandeleur's term of mourning. The deliberations of an impulsive man sometimes land him in strange countries. Ambrose Tester confided his plan to me as a tremendous secret. He professed to wish immensely to know how it appeared to me, and whether my woman's wit could n't discover for him some loophole big enough round, some honorable way of not keeping faith. Yet at the same time he seemed not to foresee that I should, of necessity, be simply horrified. Disconcerted and perplexed (a little), that he was prepared to find me; but if I had refused, as yet, to come to his assistance, he appeared to suppose it was only because of the real difficulty of suggesting to him that perfect pretext of which he was in want. He evidently counted upon me, however, for some illuminating proposal, and I think he would have liked to say to me, "You have always pretended to be a great friend of mine,"—I hadn't; the pretension was all on his side,—"and now is your chance to show it. Go to Joscelind and make her feel (women have a hundred ways of doing that sort of thing), that through Vandeleur's death the change in my situation is complete. If she is the girl I take her for, she will know what to do in the premises."

I was not prepared to oblige him to this degree, and I lost no time in telling him so, after my first surprise at seeing how definite his purpose had become. His contention, after all, was very simple. He had been in love with Lady Vandeleur for years, and was now more in love with her than ever. There had been no appearance of her being, within a calculable period, liberated by the death of her husband. This nobleman was—he didn't say what just then (it was too soon)—but he was only forty years old, and in such health and preservation as to make such a contingency infinitely remote. Under these circumstances, Ambrose had been driven, for the most worldly reasons—he was ashamed of them, pah!—into an engagement with a girl he did n't love, and did n't pretend to love. Suddenly the unexpected occurred; the woman he did love had become accessible to him, and all the relations of things were altered.

Why should n't he alter, too? Why should n't Miss Bernardstone alter, Lady Emily alter, and every one alter? It would be *wrong* in him to marry Joscelind in so changed a world;—a moment's consideration would certainly assure me of that. He could no longer carry out his part of the bargain, and the transaction must stop before it went any further. If Joscelind knew, she would be the first to recognize this, and the thing for her now was to know.

"Go and tell her, then, if you are so sure of it," I said. "I wonder you have put it off so many days."

He looked at me with a melancholy eye. "Of course I know it's beastly awkward."

It was beastly awkward certainly; there I could quite agree with him, and this was the only sympathy he extracted from me. It was impossible to be less helpful, less merciful, to an embarrassed young man than I was on that occasion. But other occasions followed very quickly, on which Mr. Tester renewed his appeal with greater eloquence. He assured me that it was torture to be with his intended, and every hour that he did n't break off committed him more deeply and more fatally. I repeated only once my previous question,—asked him only once why then he did n't tell her he had changed his mind. The inquiry was idle, was even unkind, for my young man was in a very tight place. He did n't tell her, simply because he could n't, in spite of the anguish of feeling that his chance to right himself was rapidly passing away. When I asked him if Joscelind appeared to have guessed nothing, he broke out, "How in the world can she guess, when I am so kind to her? I am so sorry for her, poor little wretch, that I can't help being nice to her. And from the moment I am nice to her she thinks it's all right."

I could see perfectly what he meant by that, and I liked him more for this little generosity than I disliked him for his nefarious scheme. In fact, I did n't dislike him at all when I saw what an influence my judgment would have on him. I very soon gave him the full benefit of it. I had thought over his case with all the advantages of his own presentation of it, and it was impossible for me to see how he could decently get rid of the girl. That, as I have said, had been my original opinion, and quickened reflection only confirmed it. As I have also said, I had n't in the least recommended him to become engaged; but once he had done so I recommended him to abide by it. It was all very well being in love with Lady Vandeleur; he might be in love with her, but he had n't promised to marry her. It was all very well not being in love with Miss Bernardstone; but, as it happened, he had promised to marry her, and in my country a gentleman was supposed to keep such promises. If it was a question of keeping them only so long as was convenient, where would any of us be? I assure you I became very eloquent and moral,—yes, moral, I maintain the word, in spite of your perhaps thinking (as you are very capable of doing) that I ought to have advised him in just the opposite sense. It was not a question of love, but of marriage, for he had never promised to love poor Joscelind. It was useless his saying it was dreadful to marry without love; he knew that he thought it, and the people he lived with thought it, nothing of the kind. Half his friends had married on those terms. "Yes, and a pretty sight their private life presented!" That might be, but it was the first time I had ever heard him say it. A fortnight before he had been quite ready to do like the others. I knew what I thought, and I suppose I expressed it with some clearness, for my arguments made him still more uncomfortable, unable as he was either to accept them or to act in contempt of them. Why he should have cared so much for my opinion is a mystery I can't elucidate; to understand my little story, you must simply swallow it. That he did care is proved by the exasperation with which he suddenly broke out, "Well, then, as I understand you, what you recommend me is to marry Miss Bernardstone, and carry on an intrigue with Lady Vandeleur!"

He knew perfectly that I recommended nothing of the sort, and he must have been very angry to indulge in this *boutade*. He told me that other people did n't think as I did—that every one was of the opinion that between a woman he did n't love and a woman he had adored for years it was a plain moral duty not to hesitate. "Don't hesitate then!" I exclaimed; but I did n't get rid of him with this, for he returned to the charge more than once (he came to me so often that I thought he must neglect both his other alternatives), and let me know again that the voice of society was quite against my view. You will doubtless be surprised at such an intimation that he had taken "society" into his confidence, and wonder whether he went about asking people whether they thought he might back out. I can't tell you exactly, but I know that for some weeks his dilemma was a great deal talked about. His friends perceived he was at the parting of the roads, and many of them had no difficulty in saying which one *they* would take. Some observers thought he ought to do nothing, to leave things as they were. Others took very high ground and discoursed upon the sanctity of love and the wickedness of really deceiving the girl, as that would be what it would amount to (if he should lead her to the altar). Some held that it was too late to escape, others maintained that it is never too late. Some thought Miss Bernardstone very much to be pitied; some reserved their compassion for Ambrose Tester; others, still, lavished it upon Lady Vandeleur.

The prevailing opinion, I think, was that he ought to obey the promptings of his heart—London cares so much for the heart! Or is it that London is simply ferocious, and always prefers the spectacle that is more entertaining? As it would prolong the drama for the young man to throw over Miss Bernardstone, there was a considerable readiness to see the poor girl sacrificed. She was like a Christian maiden in the Roman arena. That is what Ambrose Tester meant by telling me that public opinion was on his side. I don't think he chattered about his quandary, but people, knowing his situation, guessed what was going on in his mind, and he on his side guessed what they said. London discussions might as well go on in the whispering-gallery of St. Paul's. I could of course do only one thing,—I could but reaffirm my conviction that the Roman attitude, as I may call it, was cruel, was falsely sentimental. This naturally did n't help him as he wished to be helped,—did n't remove the obstacle to his marrying in a year or two Lady Vandeleur. Yet he continued to look to me for inspiration,—I must say it at the cost of making him appear a very feeble-minded gentleman. There was a moment when I thought him capable of an oblique movement, of temporizing with a view to escape. If he succeeded in postponing his marriage long enough, the Bernardstones would throw *him* over, and I suspect that for a day he entertained the idea of fixing this responsibility on them. But he was too honest and too generous to do so for longer, and his destiny was staring him in the face when an accident gave him a momentary relief. General Bernardstone died, after an illness as sudden and short as that which had carried off Lord Vandeleur; his wife and daughter were plunged into mourning and immediately retired into the country. A week later we heard that the girl's marriage would be put off for several months,—partly on account of her mourning, and partly because her mother, whose only companion she had now become, could not bear to part with her at the time originally fixed and actually so near. People of course looked at each other,—said it was the beginning of the end, a "dodge" of Ambrose Tester's. I wonder they did n't accuse him of poisoning the poor old general. I know to a certainty that he had nothing to do with the delay, that the proposal came from Lady Emily, who, in her bereavement, wished, very naturally, to keep a few months longer the child she was going to lose forever. It must be said, in justice to her prospective son-in-law, that he was capable either of resigning himself or of frankly (with however many blushes) telling Joscelind he could n't keep his agreement, but was not capable of trying to wriggle out of his difficulty. The plan of simply telling Joscelind he couldn't,—this was the one he had fixed upon as the best, and this was the one of which I remarked to him that it had a defect which should be counted against its advantages. The defect was that it would kill Joscelind on the spot.

I think he believed me, and his believing me made this unexpected respite very welcome to him. There was no knowing what might happen in the interval, and he passed a large part of it in looking for an issue. And yet, at the same time, he kept up the usual forms with the girl whom in his heart he had renounced. I was told more than once (for I had lost sight of the pair during the summer and autumn) that these forms were at times very casual, that he neglected Miss Bernardstone most flagrantly, and had quite resumed his old intimacy with Lady Vandeleur. I don't exactly know what was meant by this, for she spent the first three months of her widowhood in complete seclusion, in her own old house in Norfolk, where he certainly was not staying with her. I believe he stayed some time, for the partridge shooting, at a place a few miles off. It came to my ears that if Miss Bernardstone did n't take the hint it was because she was determined to stick to him through thick and thin. She never offered to let him off, and I was sure she never would; but I was equally sure that, strange as it may appear, he had not ceased to be nice to her. I have never exactly understood why he didn't hate her, and I am convinced that he was not a comedian in his conduct to her,—he was only a good fellow. I have spoken of the satisfaction that Sir Edmund took in his daughter-in-law that was to be; he delighted in looking at her, longed for her when she was out of his sight, and had her, with her mother, staying with him in the country for weeks together. If Ambrose was not so constantly at her side as he might have been, this deficiency was covered by his father's devotion to her, by her appearance of being already one of the family. Mr. Tester was away as he might be away if they were already married.

VI.

In October I met him at Doubleton; we spent three days there together. He was enjoying his respite, as he didn't scruple to tell me; and he talked to me a great deal—as usual—about Lady Vandeleur. He did n't mention Joscelind's name, except by implication in this assurance of how much he valued his weeks of grace.

"Do you mean to say that, under the circumstances, Lady Vandeleur is willing to marry you?"

I made this inquiry more expressively, doubtless, than before; for when we had talked of the matter then he had naturally spoken of her consent as a simple contingency. It was contingent upon the lapse of the first months of her bereavement; it was not a question he could begin to press a few days after her husband's death.

"Not immediately, of course; but if I wait, I think so." That, I remember, was his answer.

"If you wait till you get rid of that poor girl, of course."

"She knows nothing about that,—it's none of her business."

"Do you mean to say she does n't know you are engaged?"

"How should she know it, how should she believe it, when she sees how I love her?" the young man exclaimed; but he admitted afterwards that he had not deceived her, and that she rendered full justice to the motives that had determined him. He thought he could answer for it that she would marry him some day or other.

"Then she is a very cruel woman," I said, "and I should like, if you please, to hear no more about her." He protested against this, and, a month later, brought her up again, for a purpose. The purpose, you will see, was a very strange one indeed. I had then come back to town; it was the early part of December. I supposed he was hunting, with his own hounds; but he appeared one afternoon in my drawing-room and told me I should do him a great favor if I would go and see Lady Vandeleur.

"Go and see her? Where do you mean, in Norfolk?"

"She has come up to London—did n't you know it? She has a lot of business. She will be kept here till Christmas; I wish you would go."

"Why should I go?" I asked. "Won't you be kept here till Christmas too, and is n't that company enough for her?"

"Upon my word, you are cruel," he said, "and it's a great shame of you, when a man is trying to do his duty and is behaving like a saint."

"Is that what you call saintly, spending all your time with Lady Vandeleur? I will tell you whom I think a saint, if you would like to know."

"You need n't tell me; I know it better than you. I haven't a word to say against her; only she is stupid and hasn't any perceptions. If I am stopping a bit in London you don't understand why; it's as if you had n't any perceptions either! If I am here for a few days, I know what I am about."

"Why should I understand?" I asked,—not very candidly, because I should have been glad to. "It's your own affair; you know what you are about, as you say, and of course you have counted the cost."

"What cost do you mean? It's a pretty cost, I can tell you." And then he tried to explain—if I would only enter into it, and not be so suspicious. He was in London for the express purpose of breaking off.

"Breaking off what,—your engagement?"

"No, no, damn my engagement,—the other thing. My acquaintance, my relations—"

"Your intimacy with Lady Van—?" It was not very gentle, but I believe I burst out laughing. "If this is the way you break off, pray what would you do to keep up?"

He flushed, and looked both foolish and angry, for of course it was not very difficult to see my point. But he was—in a very clumsy manner of his own—trying to cultivate a good conscience, and he was getting no credit for it. "I suppose I may be allowed to look at her! It's a matter we have to talk over. One does n't drop such a friend in half an hour."

"One does n't drop her at all, unless one has the strength to make a sacrifice."

"It's easy for you to talk of sacrifice. You don't know what she is!" my visitor cried.

"I think I know what she is not. She is not a friend, as you call her, if she encourages you in the wrong, if she does n't help you. No, I have no patience with her," I declared; "I don't like her, and I won't go to see her!"

Mr. Tester looked at me a moment, as if he were too vexed to trust himself to speak. He had to make an effort not to say something rude. That effort however, he was capable of making, and though he held his hat as if he were going to walk out of the house, he ended by staying, by putting it down again, by leaning his head, with his elbows on his knees, in his hands, and groaning out that he had never heard of anything so impossible, and that he was the most wretched man in England. I was very sorry for him, and of course I told him so; but privately I did n't think he stood up to his duty as he ought. I said to him, however, that if he would give me his word of honor that he would not abandon Miss Bernardstone, there was no trouble I would n't take to be of use to him. I did n't think Lady Vandeleur *was* behaving well. He must allow me to repeat that; but if going to see her would give him any pleasure (of course there was no question of pleasure for *her*) I would go fifty times. I could n't imagine how it would help him, but I would do it as I would do anything else he asked me. He did n't give me his word of honor, but he said quietly, "*I* shall go straight; you need n't be afraid;" and as he spoke there was honor enough in his face. This left an opening, of course, for another catastrophe. There might be further postponements, and poor Lady Emily, indignant for the first time in her life, might declare that her daughter's situation had become intolerable and that they withdrew from the engagement. But this was too odious a chance, and I accepted Mr. Tester's assurance. He told me that the good I could do by going to see Lady Vandeleur was that it would cheer her up, in that dreary, big house in Upper Brook Street, where she was absolutely alone, with horrible overalls on the furniture, and newspapers—actually newspapers—on the mirrors. She was seeing no one, there was no one to see; but he knew she would see me. I asked him if she knew, then, he was to speak to me of coming, and whether I might allude to him, whether it was not too delicate. I shall never forget his answer to this, nor the tone in which he made it, blushing a little, and looking away. "Allude to me? Rather!" It was not the most fatuous speech I had ever heard; it had the effect of being the most modest; and it gave me an odd idea, and especially a new one, of the condition in which, at any time, one might be destined to find Lady Vandeleur. If she, too, were engaged in a struggle with her conscience (in this light they were an edifying pair!) it had perhaps changed her considerably, made her more approachable; and I reflected, ingeniously, that it probably had a humanizing effect upon her. Ambrose Tester did n't go away after I had told him that I would comply with his request. He lingered, fidgeting with his stick and gloves, and I perceived that he had more to tell me, and that the real reason why he wished me to go and see Lady Vandeleur was not that she had newspapers on her mirrors. He came out with it at last, for that "Rather!" of his (with the way I took it) had broken the ice.

"You say you don't think she behaved well" (he naturally wished to defend her). "But I dare say you don't understand her position. Perhaps you would n't behave any better in her place."

"It's very good of you to imagine me there!" I remarked, laughing.

"It's awkward for me to say. One doesn't want to dot one's i's to that extent."

"She would be delighted to marry you. That's not such a mystery."

"Well, she likes me awfully," Mr. Tester said, looking like a handsome child. "It's not all on one side; it's on both. That's the difficulty."

"You mean she won't let you go?—she holds you fast?"

But the poor fellow had, in delicacy, said enough, and at this he jumped up. He stood there a moment, smoothing his hat; then he broke out again: "Please do this. Let her know—make her feel. You can bring it in, you know." And here he paused, embarrassed.

"What can I bring in, Mr. Tester? That's the difficulty, as you say."

"What you told me the other day. You know. What you have told me before."

"What I have told you—?"

"That it would put an end to Joscelind! If you can't work round to it, what's the good of being—you?" And with this tribute to my powers he took his departure.

VII.

It was all very well of him to be so flattering, but I really did n't see myself talking in that manner to Lady Vandeleur. I wondered why he didn't give her this information himself, and what particular value it could have as coming from me. Then I said to myself that of course he *had* mentioned to her the truth I had impressed upon him (and which by this time he had evidently taken home), but that to enable it to produce its full effect upon Lady Yandeleur the further testimony of a witness more independent was required. There was nothing for me but to go and see her, and I went the next day, fully conscious that to execute Mr. Tester's commission I should have either to find myself very brave or to find her strangely confidential; and fully prepared, also, not to be admitted. But she received me, and the house in Upper Brook Street was as dismal as Ambrose Tester had represented it. The December fog (the afternoon was very dusky) seemed to pervade the muffled rooms, and her ladyship's pink lamplight to waste itself in the brown atmosphere. He had mentioned to me that the heir to the title (a cousin of her husband), who had left her unmolested for several months, was now taking possession of everything, so that what kept her in town was the business of her "turning out," and certain formalities connected with her dower. This was very ample, and the large provision made for her included the London house. She was very gracious on this occasion, but she certainly had remarkably little to say. Still, she was different, or at any rate (having taken that hint), I saw her differently. I saw, indeed, that I had never quite done her justice, that I had exaggerated her stiffness, attributed to her a kind of conscious grandeur which was in reality much more an accident of her appearance, of her figure, than a quality of her character. Her appearance is as grand as you know, and on the day I speak of, in her simplified mourning, under those vaguely gleaming *lambris*, she looked as beautiful as a great white lily. She is very simple and good-natured; she will never make an advance, but she will always respond to one, and I saw, that evening, that the way to get on with her was to treat her as if she were not too imposing. I saw also that, with her nun-like robes and languid eyes, she was a woman who might be immensely in love. All the same, we hadn't much to say to each other. She remarked that it was very kind of me to come, that she wondered how I could endure London at that season, that she had taken a drive and found the Park too dreadful, that she would ring for some more tea if I did n't like what she had given me. Our conversation wandered, stumbling a little, among these platitudes, but no allusion was made on either side to Ambrose Tester. Nevertheless, as I have said, she was different, though it was not till I got home that I phrased to myself what I had detected.

Then, recalling her white face, and the deeper, stranger expression of her beautiful eyes, I entertained myself with the idea that she was under the influence of "suppressed exaltation." The more I thought of her the more she appeared to me not natural; wound up, as it were, to a calmness beneath which there was a deal of agitation. This would have been nonsense if I had not, two days afterwards, received a note from her which struck me as an absolutely "exalted" production. Not superficially, of course; to the casual eye it would have been perfectly commonplace. But this was precisely its peculiarity, that Lady Vandeleur should have written me a note which had no apparent point save that she should like to see me again, a desire for which she did succeed in assigning a reason. She reminded me that she was paying no calls, and she hoped I wouldn't stand on ceremony, but come in very soon again, she had enjoyed my visit so much. We had not been on note-writing terms, and there was nothing in that visit to alter our relations; moreover, six months before, she would not have dreamed of addressing me in that way. I was doubly convinced, therefore, that she was passing through a crisis, that she was not in her normal state of nerves. Mr. Tester had not reappeared since the occasion I have described at length, and I thought it possible he had been capable of the bravery of leaving town. I had, however, no fear of meeting him in Upper Brook Street; for, according to my theory of his relations with Lady Vaudeleur, he regularly spent his evenings with her, it being clear to me that they must dine together. I could answer her note only by going to see her the next day, when I found abundant confirmation of that idea about the crisis. I must confess to you in advance that I have never really understood her behavior,—never understood why she should have taken me so suddenly—

with whatever reserves, and however much by implication merely—into her confidence. All I can say is that this is an accident to which one is exposed with English people, who, in my opinion, and contrary to common report, are the most demonstrative, the most expansive, the most gushing in the world. I think she felt rather isolated at this moment, and she had never had many intimates of her own sex. That sex, as a general thing, disapproved of her proceedings during the last few months, held that she was making Joscelind Bernardstone suffer too cruelly. She possibly felt the weight of this censure, and at all events was not above wishing some one to know that whatever injury had fallen upon the girl to whom Mr. Tester had so stupidly engaged himself, had not, so far as she was concerned, been wantonly inflicted. I was there, I was more or less aware of her situation, and I would do as well as any one else.

She seemed really glad to see me, but she was very nervous. Nevertheless, nearly half an hour elapsed, and I was still wondering whether she had sent for me only to discuss the question of how a London house whose appointments had the stamp of a debased period (it had been thought very handsome in 1850) could be "done up" without being made æsthetic. I forget what satisfaction I gave her on this point; I was asking myself how I could work round in the manner prescribed by Joscelind's intended. At the last, however, to my extreme surprise, Lady Vandeleur herself relieved me of this effort.

"I think you know Mr. Tester rather well," she remarked, abruptly, irrelevantly, and with a face' more conscious of the bearings of things than any I had ever seen her wear. On my confessing to such an acquaintance, she mentioned that Mr. Tester (who had been in London a few days—perhaps I had seen him) had left town and would n't come back for several weeks. This, for the moment, seemed to be all she had to communicate; but she sat looking at me from the corner of her sofa as if she wished me to profit in some way by the opportunity she had given me. Did she want help from outside, this proud, inscrutable woman, and was she reduced to throwing out signals of distress? Did she wish to be protected against herself,—applauded for such efforts as she had already made? I didn't rush forward, I was not precipitate, for I felt that now, surely, I should be able at my convenience o execute my commission. What concerned me was not to prevent Lady Vandeleur's marrying Mr. Tester, but to prevent Mr. Tester's marrying her. In a few moments—with the same irrelevance—she announced to me that he wished to, and asked whether I didn't know it I saw that this was my chance, and instantly, with extreme energy, I exclaimed,—

"Ah, for Heaven's sake don't listen to him! It would kill Miss Bernardstone!"

The tone of my voice made her color a little, and she repeated, "Miss Bernardstone?"

"The girl he is engaged to,—or has been,—don't you know? Excuse me, I thought every one knew."

"Of course I know he is dreadfully entangled. He was fairly hunted down." Lady Vandeleur was silent a moment, and then she added, with a strange smile, "Fancy, in such a situation, his wanting to marry me!"

"Fancy!" I replied. I was so struck with the oddity of her telling me her secrets that for the moment my indignation did not come to a head,—my indignation, I mean, at her accusing poor Lady Emily (and even the girl herself) of having "trapped" our friend. Later I said to myself that I supposed she was within her literal right in abusing her rival, if she was trying sincerely to give him up. "I don't know anything about his having been hunted down," I said; "but this I do know, Lady Vandeleur, I assure you, that if he should throw Joscelind over she would simply go out like that!" And I snapped my fingers.

Lady Vandeleur listened to this serenely enough; she tried at least to take the air of a woman who has no need of new arguments. "Do you know her very well?" she asked, as if she had been struck by my calling Miss Bernardstone by her Christian name.

"Well enough to like her very much." I was going to say "to pity her;" but I thought better of it.

"She must be a person of very little spirit. If a man were to jilt me, I don't think I should go out!" cried her ladyship with a laugh.

"Nothing is more probable than that she has not your courage or your wisdom. She may be weak, but she is passionately in love with him."

I looked straight into Lady Vandeleur's eyes as I said this, and I was conscious that it was a tolerably good description of my hostess.

"Do you think she would really die?" she asked in a moment.

"Die as if one should stab her with a knife. Some people don't believe in broken hearts," I continued. "I did n't till I knew Joscelind Bernardstone; then I felt that she had one that would n't be proof."

"One ought to live,—one ought always to live," said Lady Yandeleur; "and always to hold up one's head."

"Ah, I suppose that one ought n't to feel at all, if one wishes to be a great success."

"What do you call a great success?" she asked.

"Never having occasion to be pitied."

"Being pitied? That must be odious!" she said; and I saw that though she might wish for admiration, she would never wish for sympathy. Then, in a moment, she added that men, in her opinion, were very base,—a remark that was deep, but not, I think, very honest; that is, in so far as the purpose of it had been to give me the idea that Ambrose Tester had done nothing but press her, and she had done nothing but resist. They were very odd, the discrepancies in the statements of each of this pair; but it must be said for Lady Vandeleur that now that she had made up her mind (as I believed she had) to sacrifice herself, she really persuaded herself that she had not had a moment of weakness. She quite unbosomed herself, and I fairly assisted at her crisis. It appears that she had a conscience,—very much so, and even a high ideal of duty. She represented herself as moving heaven and earth to keep Ambrose Tester up to the mark, and you would never have guessed from what she told me that she had entertained ever so faintly the idea of marrying him. I am sure this was a dreadful perversion, but I forgave it on the score of that exaltation of which I have spoken. The things she said, and the way she said them, come back to me, and I thought that if she looked as handsome as that when she preached virtue to Mr. Tester, it was no wonder he liked the sermon to be going on perpetually.

"I dare say you know what old friends we are; but that does n't make any difference, does it? Nothing would induce me to marry him,—I have n't the smallest intention of marrying again. It is not a time for me to think of marrying, before his lordship has been dead six months. The girl is nothing to me; I know nothing about her, and I don't wish to know; but I should be very, very sorry if she were unhappy. He is the best friend I ever had, but I don't see that that's any reason I should marry him, do you?" Lady Vaudeleur appealed to me, but without waiting for my answers, asking advice in spite of herself, and then remembering it was beneath her dignity to appear to be in need of it. "I have told him that if he does n't act properly I shall never speak to him again. She's a charming girl, every one says, and I have no doubt she will make him perfectly happy. Men don't feel things like women, I think, and if they are coddled and flattered they forget the rest. I have no doubt she is very sufficient for all that. For me, at any rate, once I see a thing in a certain way, I must abide by that I think people are so dreadful,—they do such horrible things. They don't seem to think what one's duty may be. I don't know whether you think much about that, but really one must at times, don't you think so? Every one is so selfish, and then, when they have never made an effort or a sacrifice themselves, they come to you and talk such a lot of hypocrisy. I know so much better than any one else whether I should marry or not. But I don't mind telling you that I don't see why I should. I am not in such a bad position,—with my liberty and a decent maintenance."

In this manner she rambled on, gravely and communicatively, contradicting herself at times; not talking fast (she never did), but dropping one simple sentence, with an interval, after the other, with a certain richness of voice which always was part of the charm of her presence. She wished to be convinced against herself, and it was a comfort to her to hear herself argue. I was quite willing to be part of the audience, though I had to confine myself to very superficial remarks; for when I had said the event I feared would kill Miss Bernardstone I had said everything that was open to me. I had nothing to do with Lady Vandeleur's marrying, apart from that I probably disappointed her. She had caught a glimpse of the moral beauty of self-sacrifice, of a certain ideal of conduct (I imagine it was rather new to her), and would have been glad to elicit from me, as a person of some experience of life, an assurance that such joys are not insubstantial. I had no wish to wind her up to a spiritual ecstasy from which she would inevitably descend again, and I let her deliver herself according to her humor, without attempting to answer for it that she would find renunciation the road to bliss. I believed that if she should give up Mr. Tester she would suffer accordingly; but I did n't think that a reason for not giving him up. Before I left her she said to me that nothing would induce her to do anything that she did n't think right. "It would be no pleasure to me, don't you see? I should be always thinking that another way would have been better. Nothing would induce me,—nothing, nothing!"

VIII.

She protested too much, perhaps, but the event seemed to show that she was in earnest. I have described these two first visits of mine in some detail, but they were not the only ones I paid her. I saw her several times again, before she left town, and we became intimate, as London intimacies are measured. She ceased to protest (to my relief, for it made me nervous), she was very gentle, and gracious, and reasonable, and there was something in the way she looked and spoke that told me that for the present she found renunciation its own reward. So far, my scepticism was put to shame; her spiritual ecstasy maintained itself. If I could have foreseen then that it would maintain itself till the present hour I should have felt that Lady Vandeleur's moral nature is finer indeed than mine. I heard from her that Mr. Tester remained at his father's, and that Lady Emily and her daughter were also there. The day for the wedding had been fixed, and the preparations were going rapidly forward. Meanwhile—she didn't tell me, but I gathered it from things she dropped—she was in almost daily correspondence with the young man. I thought this a strange concomitant of his bridal arrangements; but apparently, henceforth, they were bent on convincing each other that the torch of virtue lighted their steps, and they couldn't convince each other too much. She intimated to me that she had now effectually persuaded him (always by letter), that he would fail terribly if he should try to found his happiness on an injury done to another, and that of course she could never be happy (in a union with him), with the sight of his wretchedness before her. That a good deal of correspondence should be required to elucidate this is perhaps after all not remarkable. One day, when I was sitting with her (it was just before she left town), she suddenly burst into tears. Before we parted I said to her that there were several women in London I liked very much,—that was common enough,—but for her I had a positive respect, and that was rare. My respect continues still, and it sometimes makes me furious.

About the middle of January Ambrose Tester reappeared in town. He told me he came to bid me good-by. He was going to be beheaded. It was no use saying that old relations would be the same after a man was married; they would be different, everything would be different. I had wanted him to marry, and now I should see how I liked it He did n't mention that I had also wanted him not to marry, and I was sure that if Lady Vandeleur had become his wife, she would have been a much greater impediment to our harmless friendship than Joscelind Bernardstone would ever be. It took me but a short time to observe that he was in very much the same condition as Lady Vandeleur. He was finding how sweet it is to renounce, hand in hand with one we love. Upon him, too, the peace of the Lord had descended. He spoke of his father's delight at the nuptials being so near at hand; at the festivities that would take place in Dorsetshire when he should bring home his bride. The only allusion he made to what we had talked of the last time we were together was to exclaim suddenly, "How can I tell you how easy she has made it? She is so sweet, so noble. She really is a perfect creature!" I took for granted that he was talking of his future wife, but in a moment, as we were at cross-purposes, perceived that he meant Lady Vandeleur. This seemed to me really ominous. It stuck in my mind after he had left me. I was half tempted to write him a note, to say, "There is, after all, perhaps, something worse than your jilting Miss Bernardstone would be; and that is the danger that your rupture with Lady Vandeleur may become more of a bond than your marrying her would have been For Heaven's sake, let your sacrifice *be* a sacrifice; keep it in its proper place!"

Of course I did n't write; even the slight responsibility I had already incurred began to frighten me, and I never saw Mr. Tester again till he was the husband of Joscelind Bernardstone. They have now been married some four years; they have two children, the eldest of whom is, as he should be, a boy. Sir Edmund waited till his grandson had made good his place in the world, and then, feeling it was safe, he quietly, genially surrendered his trust. He died, holding the hand of his daughter-in-law, and giving it doubtless a pressure which was an injunction to be brave. I don't know what he thought of the success of his plan for his son; but perhaps, after all, he saw nothing amiss, for Joscelind is the last woman in the world to have troubled him with her sorrows. From him, no doubt, she successfully concealed that bewilderment on which I have touched. You see I speak of her sorrows as if they were a matter of common recognition; certain it is that any one who meets her must see that she does n't pass her life in joy. Lady Vandeleur, as you know, has never married again; she is still the most beautiful widow in England. She enjoys the esteem of every one, as well as the approbation of her conscience, for every one knows the sacrifice she made, knows that she was even more in love with Sir Ambrose than he was with her. She goes out again, of course, as of old, and she constantly meets the baronet and his wife. She is supposed to be even "very nice" to Lady Tester, and she certainly treats her with exceeding civility. But you know (or perhaps you don't know) all the deadly things that, in London, may lie beneath that method. I don't in the least mean that Lady Vandeleur has any deadly intentions; she is a very good woman, and I am sure that in her heart she thinks she lets poor Joscelind off very easily. But the result of the whole situation is that Joscelind is in dreadful fear of her, for how can she help seeing that she has a very peculiar power over her husband? There couldn't have been a better occasion for observing the three together (if together it may be called, when Lady Tester is so completely outside), than those two days of ours at Doubleton. That's a house where they have met more than once before; I think she and Sir Ambrose like it. By "she" I mean, as he used to mean, Lady Vandeleur. You saw how Lady Tester was absolutely white with uneasiness. What can she do when she meets everywhere the implication that if two people in our time have distinguished themselves for their virtue, it is her husband and Lady Vandeleur? It is my impression that this pair are exceedingly happy. His marriage *has* made a difference, and I see him much less frequently and less intimately. But when I meet him I notice in him a kind of emanation of quiet bliss. Yes, they are certainly in felicity, they have trod the clouds together, they have soared into the blue, and they wear in their faces the glory of those altitudes. They encourage, they cheer, inspire, sustain, each other, remind each other that they have chosen the better part Of course they have to meet for this purpose, and their interviews are filled, I am sure, with its sanctity. He holds up his head, as a man may who on a very critical occasion behaved like a perfect gentleman. It is only poor Joscelind that droops. Have n't I explained to you now why she does n't understand?

FOUR MEETINGS

I saw her only four times, but I remember them vividly; she made an impression upon me. I thought her very pretty and very interesting,—a charming specimen of a type. I am very sorry to hear of her death; and yet, when I think of it, why should I be sorry? The last time I saw her she was certainly not—But I will describe all our meetings in order.

I.

The first one took place in the country, at a little tea-party, one snowy night. It must have been some seventeen years ago. My friend Latouche, going to spend Christmas with his mother, had persuaded me to go with him, and the good lady had given in our honor the entertainment of which I speak. To me it was really entertaining; I had never been in the depths of New England at that season. It had been snowing all day, and the drifts were knee-high. I wondered how the ladies had made their way to the house; but I perceived that at Grimwinter a conversazione offering the attraction of two gentlemen from New York was felt to be worth an effort.

Mrs. Latouche, in the course of the evening, asked me if I "did n't want to" show the photographs to some of the young ladies. The photographs were in a couple of great portfolios, and had been brought home by her son, who, like myself, was lately returned from Europe. I looked round and was struck with the fact that most of the young ladies were provided with an object of interest more absorbing than the most vivid sun-picture. But there was a person standing alone near the mantelshelf, and looking round the room with a small gentle smile which seemed at odds, somehow, with her isolation. I looked at her a moment, and then said, "I should like to show them to that young lady."

"Oh, yes," said Mrs. Latouche, "she is just the person. She doesn't care for flirting; I will speak to her."

I rejoined that if she did not care for flirting, she was, perhaps, not just the person; but Mrs. Latouche had already gone to propose the photographs to her.

"She's delighted," she said, coming back. "She is just the person, so quiet and so bright." And then she told me the young lady was, by name, Miss Caroline Spencer, and with this she introduced me.

Miss Caroline Spencer was not exactly a beauty, but she was a charming little figure. She must have been close upon thirty, but she was made almost like a little girl, and she had the complexion of a child. She had a very pretty head, and her hair was arranged as nearly as possible like the hair of a Greek bust, though indeed it was to be doubted if she had ever seen a Greek bust. She was "artistic," I suspected, so far as Grimwinter allowed such tendencies. She had a soft, surprised eye, and thin lips, with very pretty teeth. Round her neck she wore what ladies call, I believe, a "ruche," fastened with a very small pin in pink coral, and in her hand she carried a fan made of plaited straw and adorned with pink ribbon. She wore a scanty black silk dress. She spoke with a kind of soft precision, showing her white teeth between her narrow but tender-looking lips, and she seemed extremely pleased, even a little fluttered, at the prospect of my demonstrations. These went forward very smoothly, after I had moved the portfolios out of their corner and placed a couple of chairs near a lamp. The photographs were usually things I knew,—large views of Switzerland, Italy, and Spain, landscapes, copies of famous buildings, pictures, and statues. I said what I could about them, and my companion, looking at them as I held them up, sat perfectly still, with her straw fan raised to her underlip. Occasionally, as I laid one of the pictures down, she said very softly, "Have you seen that place?" I usually answered that I had seen it several times (I had been a great traveller), and then I felt that she looked at me askance for a moment with her pretty eyes. I had asked her at the outset whether she had been to Europe; to this she answered, "No, no, no," in a little quick, confidential whisper. But after that, though she never took her eyes off the pictures, she said so little that I was afraid she was bored. Accordingly, after we had finished one portfolio, I offered, if she desired it, to desist. I felt that she was not bored, but her reticence puzzled me, and I wished to make her speak. I turned round to look at her, and saw that there was a faint flush in each of her cheeks. She was waving her little fan to and fro. Instead of looking at me she fixed her eyes upon the other portfolio, which was leaning against the table.

"Won't you show me that?" she asked, with a little tremor in her voice. I could almost have believed she was agitated.

"With pleasure," I answered, "if you are not tired."

"No, I am not tired," she affirmed. "I like it—I love it."

And as I took up the other portfolio she laid her hand upon it, rubbing it softly.

"And have you been here too?" she asked.

On my opening the portfolio it appeared that I had been there. One of the first photographs was a large view of the Castle of Chillon, on the Lake of Geneva.

"Here," I said, "I have been many a time. Is it not beautiful?" And I pointed to the perfect reflection of the rugged rocks and pointed towers in the clear still water. She did not say, "Oh, enchanting!" and push it away to see the next picture. She looked awhile, and then she asked if it was not where Bonnivard, about whom Byron wrote, was confined. I assented, and tried to quote some of Byron's verses, but in this attempt I succeeded imperfectly.

She fanned herself a moment, and then repeated the lines correctly, in a soft, flat, and yet agreeable voice. By the time she had finished she was blushing. I complimented her and told her she was perfectly equipped for visiting Switzerland and Italy. She looked at me askance again, to see whether I was serious, and I added, that if she wished to recognize Byron's descriptions she must go abroad speedily; Europe was getting sadly dis-Byronized.

"How soon must I go?" she asked.

"Oh, I will give you ten years."

"I think I can go within ten years," she answered very soberly.

"Well," I said, "you will enjoy it immensely; you will find it very charming." And just then I came upon a photograph of some nook in a foreign city which I had been very fond of, and which recalled tender memories. I discoursed (as I suppose) with a certain eloquence; my companion sat listening, breathless.

"Have you been *very* long in foreign lands?" she asked, some time after I had ceased.

"Many years," I said.

"And have you travelled everywhere?"

"I have travelled a great deal. I am very fond of it; and, happily, I have been able."

Again she gave me her sidelong gaze. "And do you know the foreign languages?"

"After a fashion."

"Is it hard to speak them?"

"I don't believe you would find it hard," I gallantly responded.

"Oh, I shouldn't want to speak; I should only want to listen," she said. Then, after a pause, she added, "They say the French theatre is so beautiful."

"It is the best in the world."

"Did you go there very often?"

"When I was first in Paris I went every night."

"Every night!" And she opened her clear eyes very wide. "That to me is:—" and she hesitated a moment—"is very wonderful." A few minutes later she asked, "Which country do you prefer?"

"There is one country I prefer to all others. I think you would do the same."

She looked at me a moment, and then she said softly, "Italy?"

"Italy," I answered softly, too; and for a moment we looked at each other. She looked as pretty as if, instead of showing her photographs, I had been making love to her. To increase the analogy, she glanced away, blushing. There was a silence, which she broke at last by saying,—

"That is the place which, in particular, I thought of going to."

"Oh, that's the place, that's the place!" I said.

She looked at two or three photographs in silence. “They say it is not so dear.”

“As some other countries? Yes, that is not the least of its charms.”

“But it is all very dear, is it not?”

“Europe, you mean?”

“Going there and travelling. That has been the trouble. I have very little money. I give lessons,” said Miss Spencer.

“Of course one must have money,” I said, “but one can manage with a moderate amount.”

“I think I should manage. I have laid something by, and I am always adding a little to it. It’s all for that.” She paused a moment, and then went on with a kind of suppressed eagerness, as if telling me the story were a rare, but a possibly impure satisfaction, “But it has not been only the money; it has been everything. Everything has been against it I have waited and waited. It has been a mere castle in the air. I am almost afraid to talk about it. Two or three times it has been a little nearer, and then I have talked about it and it has melted away. I have talked about it too much,” she said hypocritically; for I saw that such talking was now a small tremulous ecstasy. “There is a lady who is a great friend of mine; she does n’t want to go; I always talk to her about it. I tire her dreadfully. She told me once she did n’t know what would become of me. I should go crazy if I did not go to Europe, and I should certainly go crazy if I did.”

“Well,” I said, “you have not gone yet, and nevertheless you are not crazy.”

She looked at me a moment, and said, “I am not so sure. I don’t think of anything else. I am always thinking of it. It prevents me from thinking of things that are nearer home, things that I ought to attend to. That is a kind of craziness.”

“The cure for it is to go,” I said.

“I have a faith that I shall go. I have a cousin in Europe!” she announced.

We turned over some more photographs, and I asked her if she had always lived at Grimwinter.

"Oh, no, sir," said Miss Spencer. "I have spent twenty-three months in Boston."

I answered, jocosely, that in that case foreign lands would probably prove a disappointment to her; but I quite failed to alarm her.

"I know more about them than you might think," she said, with her shy, neat little smile. "I mean by reading; I have read a great deal I have not only read Byron; I have read histories and guidebooks. I know I shall like it."

"I understand your case," I rejoined. "You have the native American passion,—the passion for the picturesque. With us, I think it is primordial,—antecedent to experience. Experience comes and only shows us something we have dreamt of."

"I think that is very true," said Caroline Spencer. "I have dreamt of everything; I shall know it all!"

"I am afraid you have wasted a great deal of time."

"Oh, yes, that has been my great wickedness."

The people about us had begun to scatter; they were taking their leave. She got up and put out her hand to me, timidly, but with a peculiar brightness in her eyes.

"I am going back there," I said, as I shook hands with her. "I shall look out for you."

"I will tell you," she answered, "if I am disappointed."

And she went away, looking delicately agitated, and moving her little straw fan.

II.

A few months after this I returned to Europe, and some three years elapsed. I had been living in Paris, and, toward the end of October, I went from that city to Havre, to meet my sister and her husband, who had written me that they were about to arrive there. On reaching Havre I found that the steamer was already in; I was nearly two hours late. I repaired directly to the hotel, where my relatives were already established. My sister had gone to bed, exhausted and disabled by her voyage; she was a sadly incompetent sailor, and her sufferings on this occasion had been extreme. She wished, for the moment, for undisturbed rest, and was unable to see me more than five minutes; so it was agreed that we should remain at Havre until the next day. My brother-in-law, who was anxious about his wife, was unwilling to leave her room; but she insisted upon his going out with me to take a walk and recover his landlegs. The early autumn day was warm and charming, and our stroll through the bright-colored, busy streets of the old French seaport was sufficiently entertaining. We walked along the sunny, noisy quays, and then turned into a wide, pleasant street, which lay half in sun and half in shade—a French provincial street, that looked like an old water-color drawing: tall, gray, steep-roofed, red-gabled, many-storied houses; green shutters on windows and old scroll-work above them; flower-pots in balconies, and white-capped women in doorways. We walked in the shade; all this stretched away on the sunny side of the street and made a picture. We looked at it as we passed along; then, suddenly, my brother-in-law stopped, pressing my arm and staring. I followed his gaze and saw that we had paused just before coming to a *café*, where, under an awning, several tables and chairs were disposed upon the pavement The windows were open behind; half a dozen plants in tubs were ranged beside the door; the pavement was besprinkled with clean bran. It was a nice little, quiet, old-fashioned *café*; inside, in the comparative dusk, I saw a stout, handsome woman, with pink ribbons in her cap, perched up with a mirror behind her back, smiling at some one who was out of sight. All this, however, I perceived afterwards; what I first observed was a lady sitting alone, outside, at one of the little marble-topped tables. My brother-in-law had stopped to look at her. There was something on the little table, but she was leaning back quietly, with her hands folded, looking down the street, away from us. I saw her only in something less than profile; nevertheless, I instantly felt that I had seen her before.

"The little lady of the steamer!" exclaimed my brother-in-law.

"Was she on your steamer?" I asked.

"From morning till night She was never sick. She used to sit perpetually at the side of the vessel with her hands crossed that way, looking at the eastward horizon."

"Are you going to speak to her?"

"I don't know her. I never made acquaintance with her. I was too seedy. But I used to watch her and—I don't know why—to be interested in her. She's a dear little Yankee woman. I have an idea she is a schoolmistress taking a holiday, for which her scholars have made up a purse."

She turned her face a little more into profile, looking at the steep gray house-fronts opposite to her. Then I said, "I shall speak to her myself."

"I would n't; she is very shy," said my brother-in-law.

"My dear fellow, I know her. I once showed her photographs at a tea-party."

And I went up to her. She turned and looked at me, and I saw she was in fact Miss Caroline Spencer. But she was not so quick to recognize me; she looked startled. I pushed a chair to the table and sat down.

"Well," I said, "I hope you are not disappointed!"

She stared, blushing a little; then she gave a small jump which betrayed recognition.

"It was you who showed me the photographs, at Grimwinter!"

"Yes, it was I. This happens very charmingly, for I feel as if it were for me to give you a formal reception here, an official welcome. I talked to you so much about Europe."

"You did n't say too much. I am so happy!" she softly exclaimed.

Very happy she looked. There was no sign of her being older; she was as gravely, decently, demurely pretty as before. If she had seemed before a thin-stemmed, mild-hued flower of Puritanism, it may be imagined whether in her present situation this delicate bloom was less apparent. Beside her an old gentleman was drinking absinthe; behind her the *dame de comptoir* in the pink ribbons was calling "Alcibiade! Alcibiade!" to the long-aproned waiter. I explained to Miss Spencer that my companion had lately been her shipmate, and my brother-in-law came up and was introduced to her. But she looked at him as if she had never seen him before, and I remembered that he had told me that her eyes were always fixed upon the eastward horizon. She had evidently not noticed him, and, still timidly smiling, she made no attempt whatever to pretend that she had. I stayed with her at the *café* door, and he went back to the hotel and to his wife. I said to Miss Spencer that this meeting of ours in the first hour of her landing was really very strange, but that I was delighted to be there and receive her first impressions.

"Oh, I can't tell you," she said; "I feel as if I were in a dream. I have been sitting here for an hour, and I don't want to move. Everything is so picturesque. I don't know whether the coffee has intoxicated me; it 's so delicious."

"Really," said I, "if you are so pleased with this poor prosaic Havre, you will have no admiration left for better things. Don't spend your admiration all the first day; remember it's your intellectual letter of credit. Remember all the beautiful places and things that are waiting for you; remember that lovely Italy!"

"I 'm not afraid of running short," she said gayly, still looking at the opposite houses. "I could sit here all day, saying to myself that here I am at last. It's so dark and old and different."

"By the way," I inquired, "how come you to be sitting here? Have you not gone to one of the inns?" For I was half amused, half alarmed, at the good conscience with which this delicately pretty woman had stationed herself in conspicuous isolation on the edge of the *trottoir*.

"My cousin brought me here," she answered. "You know I told you I had a cousin in Europe. He met me at the steamer this morning."

"It was hardly worth his while to meet you if he was to desert you so soon."

"Oh, he has only left me for half an hour," said Miss Spencer. "He has gone to get my money."

"Where is your money?"

She gave a little laugh. "It makes me feel very fine to tell you! It is in some circular notes."

"And where are your circular notes?"

"In my cousin's pocket."

This statement was very serenely uttered, but—I can hardly say why—it gave me a sensible chill At the moment I should have been utterly unable to give the reason of this sensation, for I knew nothing of Miss Spencer's cousin. Since he was her cousin, the presumption was in his favor. But I felt suddenly uncomfortable at the thought that, half an hour after her landing, her scanty funds should have passed into his hands.

"Is he to travel with you?" I asked.

"Only as far as Paris. He is an art-student, in Paris. I wrote to him that I was coming, but I never expected him to come off to the ship. I supposed he would only just meet me at the train in Paris. It is very kind of him. But he *is* very kind, and very bright."

I instantly became conscious of an extreme curiosity to see this bright cousin who was an art-student.

"He is gone to the banker's?" I asked.

"Yes, to the banker's. He took me to a hotel, such a queer, quaint, delicious little place, with a court in the middle, and a gallery all round, and a lovely landlady, in such a beautifully fluted cap, and such a perfectly fitting dress! After a while we came out to walk to the banker's, for I haven't got any French money. But I was very dizzy from the motion of the vessel, and I thought I had better sit down. He found this place for me here, and he went off to the banker's himself. I am to wait here till he comes back."

It may seem very fantastic, but it passed through my mind that he would never come back. I settled myself in my chair beside Miss Spencer and determined to await the event. She was extremely observant; there was something touching in it. She noticed everything that the movement of the street brought before us,—peculiarities of costume, the shapes of vehicles, the big Norman horses, the fat priests, the shaven poodles. We talked of these things, and there was something charming in her freshness of perception and the way her book-nourished fancy recognized and welcomed everything.

"And when your cousin comes back, what are you going to do?" I asked.

She hesitated a moment. "We don't quite know."

"When do you go to Paris? If you go by the four o'clock train, I may have the pleasure of making the journey with you."

"I don't think we shall do that. My cousin thinks I had better stay here a few days."

"Oh!" said I; and for five minutes said nothing more. I was wondering what her cousin was, in vulgar parlance, "up to." I looked up and down the street, but saw nothing that looked like a bright American art-student. At last I took the liberty of observing that Havre was hardly a place to choose as one of the æsthetic stations of a European tour. It was a place of convenience, nothing more; a place of transit, through which transit should be rapid. I recommended her to go to Paris by the afternoon train, and meanwhile to amuse herself by driving to the ancient fortress at the mouth of the harbor,—that picturesque circular structure which bore the name of Francis the First, and looked like a small castle of St. Angelo. (It has lately been demolished.)

She listened with much interest; then for a moment she looked grave.

"My cousin told me that when he returned he should have something particular to say to me, and that we could do nothing or decide nothing until I should have heard it. But I will make him tell me quickly, and then we will go to the ancient fortress. There is no hurry to get to Paris; there is plenty of time."

She smiled with her softly severe little lips as she spoke those last words. But I, looking at her with a purpose, saw just a tiny gleam of apprehension in her eye.

"Don't tell me," I said, "that this wretched man is going to give you bad news!"

"I suspect it is a little bad, but I don't believe it is very bad. At any rate, I must listen to it."

I looked at her again an instant. "You did n't come to Europe to listen," I said. "You came to see!" But now I was sure her cousin would come back; since he had something disagreeable to say to her, he certainly would turn up. We sat a while longer, and I asked her about her plans of travel She had them on her fingers' ends, and she told over the names with a kind of solemn distinctness: from Paris to Dijon and to Avignon, from Avignon to Marseilles and the Cornice road; thence to Genoa, to Spezia, to Pisa, to Florence, to Home. It apparently had never occurred to her that there could be the least incommodity in her travelling alone; and since she was unprovided with a companion I of course scrupulously abstained from disturbing her sense of security. At last her cousin came back. I saw him turn towards us out of a side street, and from the moment my eyes rested upon him I felt that this was the bright American art-student. He wore a slouch hat and a rusty black velvet jacket, such as I had often encountered in the Rue Bonaparte. His shirt-collar revealed the elongation of a throat which, at a distance, was not strikingly statuesque. He was tall and lean; he had red hair and freckles. So much I had time to observe while he approached the *café*, staring at me with natural surprise from under his umbrageous coiffure. When he came up to us I immediately introduced myself to him as an old acquaintance of Miss Spencer. He looked at me hard with a pair of little red eyes, then he made me a solemn bow in the French fashion, with his sombrero.

"You were not on the ship?" he said.

"No, I was not on the ship. I have been in Europe these three years."

He bowed once more, solemnly, and motioned me to be seated again. I sat down, but it was only for the purpose of observing him an instant; I saw it was time I should return to my sister. Miss Spencer's cousin was a queer fellow. Nature had not shaped him for a Raphaelesque or Byronic attire, and his velvet doublet and naked neck were not in harmony with his facial attributes. His hair was cropped close to his head; his ears were large and ill-adjusted to the same. He had a lackadaisical carriage and a sentimental droop which were peculiarly at variance with his keen, strange-colored eyes. Perhaps I was prejudiced, but I thought his eyes treacherous. He said nothing for some time; he leaned his hands on his cane and looked up and down the street Then at last, slowly lifting his cane and pointing with it, "That's a very nice bit," he remarked, softly. He had his head on one side, and his little eyes were half closed. I followed the direction of his stick; the object it indicated was a red cloth hung out of an old window. "Nice bit of color," he continued; and without moving his head he transferred his half-closed gaze to me. "Composes well," he pursued. "Make a nice thing." He spoke in a hard vulgar voice.

"I see you have a great deal of eye," I replied. "Your cousin tells me you are studying art." He looked at me in the same way without answering, and I went on with deliberate urbanity, "I suppose you are at the studio of one of those great men."

Still he looked at me, and then he said softly, "Gérôme."

"Do you like it?" I asked.

"Do you understand French?" he said.

"Some kinds," I answered.

He kept his little eyes on me; then he said, "J'adore la peinture!"

"Oh, I understand that kind!" I rejoined. Miss Spencer laid her hand upon her cousin's arm with a little pleased and fluttered movement; it was delightful to be among people who were on such easy terms with foreign tongues. I got up to take leave, and asked Miss Spencer where, in Paris, I might have the honor of waiting upon her. To what hotel would she go?

She turned to her cousin inquiringly, and he honored me again with his little languid leer. "Do you know the Hôtel des Princes?"

"I know where it is."

"I shall take her there."

"I congratulate you," I said to Caroline Spencer. "I believe it is the best inn in the world; and in case I should still have a moment to call upon you here, where are you lodged?"

"Oh, it's such a pretty name," said Miss Spencer gleefully. "À la Belle Normande."

As I left them her cousin gave me a great flourish with his picturesque hat.

III.

My sister, as it proved, was not sufficiently restored to leave Havre by the afternoon train; so that, as the autumn dusk began to fall, I found myself at liberty to call at the sign of the Fair Norman. I must confess that I had spent much of the interval in wondering what the disagreeable thing was that my charming friend's disagreeable cousin had been telling her. The "Belle Normande" was a modest inn in a shady bystreet, where it gave me satisfaction to think Miss Spencer must have encountered local color in abundance. There was a crooked little court, where much of the hospitality of the house was carried on; there was a staircase climbing to bedrooms on the outer side of the wall; there was a small trickling fountain with a stucco statuette in the midst of it; there was a little boy in a white cap and apron cleaning copper vessels at a conspicuous kitchen door; there was a chattering landlady, neatly laced, arranging apricots and grapes into an artistic pyramid upon a pink plate. I looked about, and on a green bench outside of an open door labelled *Salle à Manger*, I perceived Caroline Spencer. No sooner had I looked at her than I saw that something had happened since the morning. She was leaning back on her bench, her hands were clasped in her lap, and her eyes were fixed upon the landlady, at the other side of the court, manipulating her apricots.

But I saw she was not thinking of apricots. She was staring absently, thoughtfully; as I came near her I perceived that she had been crying. I sat down on the bench beside her before she saw me; then, when she had done so, she simply turned round, without surprise, and rested her sad eyes upon me. Something very bad indeed had happened; she was completely changed.

I immediately charged her with it. "Your cousin has been giving you bad news; you are in great distress."

For a moment she said nothing, and I supposed that she was afraid to speak, lest her tears should come back. But presently I perceived that in the short time that had elapsed since my leaving her in the morning she had shed them all, and that she was now softly stoical, intensely composed.

"My poor cousin is in distress," she said at last. "His news was bad." Then, after a brief hesitation, "He was in terrible want of money."

"In want of yours, you mean?"

"Of any that he could get—honestly. Mine was the only money."

"And he has taken yours?"

She hesitated again a moment, but her glance, meanwhile, was pleading. "I gave him what I had."

I have always remembered the accent of those words as the most angelic bit of human utterance I had ever listened to; but then, almost with a sense of personal outrage, I jumped up. "Good heavens!" I said, "do you call that getting, it honestly?"

I had gone too far; she blushed deeply. "We will not speak of it," she said.

"We *must* speak of it," I answered, sitting down again. "I am your friend; it seems to me you need one. What is the matter with your cousin?"

"He is in debt."

"No doubt! But what is the special fitness of your paying his debts?"

"He has told me all his story; I am very sorry for him."

"So am I! But I hope he will give you back your money."

"Certainly he will; as soon as he can."

"When will that be?"

"When he has finished his great picture."

"My dear young lady, confound his great picture! Where is this desperate cousin?"

She certainly hesitated now. Then,—"At his dinner," she answered.

I turned about and looked through the open door into the *salle à manger*. There, alone at the end of a long table, I perceived the object of Miss Spencer's compassion, the bright young art-student. He was dining too attentively to notice me at first; but in the act of setting down a well-emptied wineglass he caught sight of my observant attitude. He paused in his repast, and, with his head on one side and his meagre jaws slowly moving, fixedly returned my gaze. Then the landlady came lightly brushing by with her pyramid of apricots.

"And that nice little plate of fruit is for him?" I exclaimed.

Miss Spencer glanced at it tenderly. "They do that so prettily!" she murmured.

I felt helpless and irritated. "Come now, really," I said; "do you approve of that long strong fellow accepting your funds?" She looked away from me; I was evidently giving her pain. The case was hopeless; the long strong fellow had "interested" her.

"Excuse me if I speak of him so unceremoniously," I said. "But you are really too generous, and he is not quite delicate enough. He made his debts himself; he ought to pay them himself."

"He has been foolish," she answered; "I know that He has told me everything. We had a long talk this morning; the poor fellow threw himself upon my charity. He has signed notes to a large amount."

"The more fool he!"

"He is in extreme distress; and it is not only himself. It is his poor wife."

"Ah, he has a poor wife?"

"I didn't know it; but he confessed everything. He married two years since, secretly."

"Why secretly?"

Caroline Spencer glanced about her, as if she feared listeners. Then softly, in a little impressive tone,—"She was a countess!"

"Are you very sure of that?"

"She has written me a most beautiful letter."

"Asking you for money, eh?"

"Asking me for confidence and sympathy," said Miss Spencer. "She has been disinherited by her father. My cousin told me the story, and she tells it in her own way, in the letter. It is like an old romance. Her father opposed the marriage, and when he discovered that she had secretly disobeyed him he cruelly cast her off. It is really most romantic. They are the oldest family in Provence."

I looked and listened in wonder. It really seemed that the poor woman was enjoying the "romance" of having a discarded countess-cousin, out of Provence, so deeply as almost to lose the sense of what the forfeiture of her money meant for her.

"My dear young lady," I said, "you don't want to be ruined for picturesqueness' sake?"

"I shall not be ruined. I shall come back before long to stay with them. The Countess insists upon that."

"Come back! You are going home, then?"

She sat for a moment with her eyes lowered, then with an heroic suppression of a faint tremor of the voice,—"I have no money for travelling!" she answered.

"You gave it *all* up?"

"I have kept enough to take me home."

I gave an angry groan; and at this juncture Miss Spencer's cousin, the fortunate possessor of her sacred savings and of the hand of the Provençal countess, emerged from the little dining-room. He stood on the threshold for an instant, removing the stone from a plump apricot which he had brought away from the table; then he put the apricot into his mouth, and while he let it sojourn there, gratefully, stood looking at us, with his long legs apart and his hands dropped into the pockets of his velvet jacket. My companion got up, giving him a thin glance which I caught in its passage, and which expressed a strange commixture of resignation and fascination,—a sort of perverted exaltation. Ugly, vulgar, pretentious, dishonest, as I thought the creature, he had appealed successfully to her eager and tender imagination. I was deeply disgusted, but I had no warrant to interfere, and at any rate I felt that it would be vain.

The young man waved his hand with a pictorial gesture. "Nice old court," he observed. "Nice mellow old place. Good tone in that brick. Nice crooked old staircase."

Decidedly, I could n't stand it; without responding I gave my hand to Caroline Spencer. She looked at me an instant with her little white face and expanded eyes, and as she showed her pretty teeth I suppose she meant to smile.

"Don't be sorry for me," she said, "I am very sure I shall see something of this dear old Europe yet."

I told her that I would not bid her goodby; I should find a moment to come back the next morning. Her cousin, who had put on his sombrero again, flourished it off at me by way of a bow, upon which I took my departure.

The next morning I came back to the inn, where I met in the court the landlady, more loosely laced than in the evening. On my asking for Miss Spencer,—"*Partie*, monsieu," said the hostess. "She went away last night at ten o 'clock, with her—her—not her husband, eh?—in fine, her *monsieur*. They went down to the American ship." I turned away; the poor girl had been about thirteen hours in Europe.

IV.

I myself, more fortunate, was there some five years longer. During this period I lost my friend Latouche, who died of a malarious fever during a tour in the Levant. One of the first things I did on my return was to go up to Grimwinter to pay a consolatory visit to his poor mother. I found her in deep affliction, and I sat with her the whole of the morning that followed my arrival (I had come in late at night), listening to her tearful descant and singing the praises of my friend. We talked of nothing else, and our conversation terminated only with the arrival of a quick little woman who drove herself up to the door in a "carryall," and whom I saw toss the reins upon the horse's back with the briskness of a startled sleeper throwing back the bed-clothes. She jumped out of the carryall and she jumped into the room. She proved to be the minister's wife and the great town-gossip, and she had evidently, in the latter capacity, a choice morsel to communicate. I was as sure of this as I was that poor Mrs. Latouche was not absolutely too bereaved to listen to her. It seemed to me discreet to retire; I said I believed I would go and take a walk before dinner.

"And, by the way," I added, "if you will tell me where my old friend Miss Spencer lives, I will walk to her house."

The minister's wife immediately responded. Miss Spencer lived in the fourth house beyond the "Baptist church; the Baptist church was the one on the right, with that queer green thing over the door; they called it a portico, but it looked more like an old-fashioned bedstead.

"Yes, do go and see poor Caroline," said Mrs. Latouche. "It will refresh her to see a strange face."

"I should think she had had enough of strange faces!" cried the minister's wife.

"I mean, to see a visitor," said Mrs. Latouche, amending her phrase.

"I should think she had had enough of visitors!" her companion rejoined. "But *you* don't mean to stay ten years," she added, glancing at me.

"Has she a visitor of that sort?" I inquired, perplexed.

"You will see the sort!" said the minister's wife. "She's easily seen; she generally sits in the front yard. Only take care what you say to her, and be very sure you are polite."

"Ah, she is so sensitive?"

The minister's wife jumped up and dropped me a curtsey, a most ironical curtsey.

"That's what she is, if you please. She's a countess!"

And pronouncing this word with the most scathing accent, the little woman seemed fairly to laugh in the Countess's face. I stood a moment, staring, wondering, remembering.

"Oh, I shall be very polite!" I cried; and grasping my hat and stick, I went on my way.

I found Miss Spencer's residence without difficulty. The Baptist church was easily identified, and the small dwelling near it, of a rusty white, with a large central chimney-stack and a Virginia creeper, seemed naturally and properly the abode of a frugal old maid with a taste for the picturesque. As I approached I slackened my pace, for I had heard that some one was always sitting in the front yard, and I wished to reconnoitre. I looked cautiously over the low white fence which separated the small garden-space from the unpaved street; but I descried nothing in the shape of a countess. A small straight path led up to the crooked doorstep, and on either side of it was a little grass-plot, fringed with currant-bushes. In the middle of the grass, on either side, was a large quince-tree, full of antiquity and contortions, and beneath one of the quince-trees were placed a small table and a couple of chairs. On the table lay a piece of unfinished embroidery and two or three books in bright-colored paper covers. I went in at the gate and paused halfway along the path, scanning the place for some farther token of its occupant, before whom—I could hardly have said why—I hesitated abruptly to present myself. Then I saw that the poor little house was very shabby. I felt a sudden doubt of my right to intrude; for curiosity had been my motive, and curiosity here seemed singularly indelicate. While I hesitated, a figure appeared in the open doorway and stood there looking at me. I immediately recognized Caroline Spencer, but she looked at me as if she had never seen me before. Gently, but gravely and timidly, I advanced to the doorstep, and then I said, with an attempt at friendly badinage,—

"I waited for you over there to come back, but you never came."

"Waited where, sir?" she asked softly, and her light-colored eyes expanded more than before.

She was much older; she looked tired and wasted.

"Well," I said, "I waited at Havre."

She stared; then she recognized me. She smiled and blushed and clasped her two hands together. "I remember you now," she said. "I remember that day." But she stood there, neither coming out nor asking me to come in. She was embarrassed.

I, too, felt a little awkward. I poked my stick into the path. "I kept looking out for you, year after year," I said.

"You mean in Europe?" murmured Miss Spencer.

"In Europe, of course! Here, apparently, you are easy enough to find."

She leaned her hand against the unpainted doorpost, and her head fell a little to one side. She looked at me for a moment without speaking, and I thought I recognized the expression that one sees in women's eyes when tears are rising. Suddenly she stepped out upon the cracked slab of stone before the threshold and closed the door behind her. Then she began to smile intently, and I saw that her teeth were as pretty as ever. But there had been tears too.

"Have you been there ever since?" she asked, almost in a whisper.

"Until three weeks ago. And you—you never came back?"

Still looking at me with her fixed smile, she put her hand behind her and opened the door again. "I am not very polite," she said. "Won't you come in?"

"I am afraid I incommode you."

"Oh, no!" she answered, smiling more than ever. And she pushed back the door, with a sign that I should enter.

I went in, following her. She led the way to a small room on the left of the narrow hall, which I supposed to be her parlor, though it was at the back of the house, and we passed the closed door of another apartment which apparently enjoyed a view of the quince-trees. This one looked out upon a small woodshed and two clucking hens. But I thought it very pretty, until I saw that its elegance was of the most frugal kind; after which, presently, I thought it prettier still, for I had never seen faded chintz and old mezzotint engravings, framed in varnished autumn leaves, disposed in so graceful a fashion. Miss Spencer sat down on a very small portion of the sofa, with her hands tightly clasped in her lap. She looked ten years older, and it would have souuded very perverse now to speak of her as pretty. But I thought her so; or at least I thought her touching. She was peculiarly agitated. I tried to appear not to notice it; but suddenly, in the most inconsequent fashion,—it was an irresistible memory of our little friendship at Havre,—I said to her, "I do incommode you. You are distressed."

She raised her two hands to her face, and for a moment kept it buried in them. Then, taking them away,—"It's because you remind me—" she said.

"I remind you, you mean, of that miserable day at Havre?"

She shook her head. "It was not miserable. It was delightful."

"I never was so shocked as when, on going back to your inn the next morning, I found you had set sail again."

She was silent a moment; and then she said, "Please let us not speak of that."

"Did you come straight back here?" I asked.

"I was back here just thirty days after I had gone away."

"And here you have remained ever since?"

"Oh, yes!" she said gently.

"When are you going to Europe again?"

This question seemed brutal; but there was something that irritated me in the softness of her resignation, and I wished to extort from her some expression of impatience.

She fixed her eyes for a moment upon a small sunspot on the carpet; then she got up and lowered the window-blind a little, to obliterate it. Presently, in the same mild voice, answering my question, she said, "Never!"

"I hope your cousin repaid you your money."

"I don't care for it now," she said, looking away from me.

"You don't care for your money?"

"For going to Europe."

"Do you mean that you would not go if you could?"

"I can't—I can't," said Caroline Spencer. "It is all over; I never think of it."

"He never repaid you, then!" I exclaimed.

"Please—please," she began.

But she stopped; she was looking toward the door. There had been a rustling aud a sound of steps in the hall.

I also looked toward the door, which was open, and now admitted another person, a lady, who paused just within the threshold. Behind her came a young man. The lady looked at me with a good deal of fixedness, long enough for my glance to receive a vivid impression of herself. Then she turned to Caroline Spencer, and, with a smile and a strong foreign accent,—

"Excuse my interruption!" she said. "I knew not you had company, the gentleman came in so quietly."

With this she directed her eyes toward me again.

She was very strange; yet my first feeling was that I had seen her before. Then I perceived that I had only seen ladies who were very much like her. But I had seen them very far away from Grimwinter, and it was an odd sensation to be seeing her here. Whither was it the sight of her seemed to transport me? To some dusky landing before a shabby Parisian *quatrième*,—to an open door revealing a greasy antechamber, and to Madame leaning over the banisters, while she holds a faded dressing-gown together and bawls down to the portress to bring up her coffee. Miss Spencer's visitor was a very large woman, of middle age, with a plump, dead-white face, and hair drawn back *a la chinoise*. She had a small penetrating eye, and what is called in French an agreeable smile. She wore an old pink cashmere dressing-gown, covered with white embroideries, and, like the figure in my momentary vision, she was holding it together in front with a bare and rounded arm and a plump and deeply dimpled hand.

"It is only to spick about my *café*," she said to Miss Spencer, with her agreeable smile. "I should like it served in the garden under the leetle tree."

The young man behind her had now stepped into the room, and he also stood looking at me. He was a pretty-faced little fellow, with an air of provincial foppishness,—a tiny Adonis of Grimwinter. He had a small pointed nose, a small pointed chin, and, as I observed, the most diminutive feet. He looked at me foolishly, with his mouth open.

"You shall have your coffee," said Miss Spencer, who had a faint red spot in each of her cheeks.

"It is well!" said the lady in the dressing-gown. "Find your bouk," she added, turning to the young man.

He gazed vaguely round the room. "My grammar, d 'ye mean?" he asked, with a helpless intonation.

But the large lady was inspecting me, curiously, and gathering in her dressing-gown with her white arm.

"Find your bouk, my friend," she repeated.

"My poetry, d 'ye mean?" said the young man, also staring at me again.

"Never mind your bouk," said his companion. "To-day we will talk. We will make some conversation. But we must not interrupt. Come;" and she turned away. "Under the leetle tree," she added, for the benefit of Miss Spencer.

Then she gave me a sort of salutation, and a "Monsieur!" with which she swept away again, followed by the young man.

Caroline Spencer stood there with her eyes fixed upon the ground.

"Who is that?" I asked.

"The Countess, my cousin."

"And who is the young man?"

"Her pupil, Mr. Mixter."

This description of the relation between the two persons who had just left the room made me break into a little laugh. Miss Spencer looked at me gravely.

"She gives French lessons; she has lost her fortune."

"I see," I said. "She is determined to be a burden to no one. That is very proper."

Miss Spencer looked down on the ground again, "I must go and get the coffee," she said.

"Has the lady many pupils?" I asked.

"She has only Mr. Mixter. She gives all her time to him."

At this I could not laugh, though I smelt provocation; Miss Spencer was too grave. "He pays very well," she presently added, with simplicity. "He is very rich. He is very kind. He takes the Countess to drive." And she was turning away.

"You are going for the Countess's coffee?" I said.

"If you will excuse me a few moments."

"Is there no one else to do it?"

She looked at me with the softest serenity. "I keep no servants."

"Can she not wait upon herself?"

"She is not used to that."

"I see," said I, as gently as possible. "But before you go, tell me this: who is this lady?"

"I told you about her before—that day. She is the wife of my cousin, whom you saw."

"The lady who was disowned by her family in consequence of her marriage?"

"Yes; they have never seen her again. They have cast her off."

"And where is her husband?"

"He is dead."

"And where is your money?"

The poor girl flinched; there was something too consistent in my questions. "I don't know," she said wearily.

But I continued a moment. "On her husband's death this lady came over here?"

"Yes, she arrived one day."

"How long ago?"

"Two years."

"She has been here ever since?"

"Every moment."

"How does she like it?"

"Not at all."

"And how do *you* like it?"

Miss Spencer laid her face in her two hands an instant, as she had done ten minutes before.

Then, quickly, she went to get the Countess's coffee.

I remained alone in the little parlor; I wanted to see more, to learn more. At the end of five minutes the young man whom Miss Spencer had described as the Countess's pupil came in. He stood looking at me for a moment with parted lips. I saw he was a very rudimentary young man.

"She wants to know if you won't come out there," he observed at last.

"Who wants to know?"

"The Countess. That French lady."

"She has asked you to bring me?"

"Yes, sir," said the young man feebly, looking at my six feet of stature.

I went out with him, and we found the Countess sitting under one of the little quince-trees in front of the house. She was drawing a needle through the piece of embroidery which she had taken from the small table. She pointed graciously to the chair beside her, and I seated myself. Mr. Mixter glanced about him, and then sat down in the grass at her feet. He gazed upward, looking with parted lips from the Countess to me. "I am sure you speak French," said the Countess, fixing her brilliant little eyes upon me.

"I do, madam, after a fashion," I answered in the lady's own tongue.

"*Voilà!*" she cried most expressively. "I knew it so soon as I looked at you. You have been in my poor dear country."

"A long time."

"You know Paris?"

"Thoroughly, madam." And with a certain conscious purpose I let my eyes meet her own.

She presently, hereupon, moved her own and glanced down at Mr. Mixter "What are we talking about?" she demanded of her attentive pupil.

He pulled his knees up, plucked at the grass with his hand, stared, blushed a little. "You are talking French," said Mr. Mixter.

"*La belle découverte!*" said the Countess. "Here are ten months," she explained to me, "that I am giving him lessons. Don't put yourself out not to say he's an idiot; he won't understand you."

"I hope your other pupils are more gratifying," I remarked.

"I have no others. They don't know what French is in this place; they don't want to know. You may therefore imagine the pleasure it is to me to meet a person who speaks it like yourself." I replied that my own pleasure was not less; and she went on drawing her stitches through her embroidery, with her little finger curled out. Every few moments she put her eyes close to her work, nearsightedly. I thought her a very disagreeable person; she was coarse, affected, dishonest, and no more a countess than I was a caliph. "Talk to me of Paris," she went on. "The very name of it gives me an emotion! How long since you were there?"

"Two months ago."

"Happy man! Tell me something about it What were they doing? Oh, for an hour of the boulevard!"

"They were doing about what they are always doing,—amusing themselves a good deal."

"At the theatres, eh?" sighed the Countess. "At the *cafés-concerts*, at the little tables in front of the doors? *Quelle existence!* You know I am a Parisienne, monsieur," she added, "to my fingertips."

"Miss Spencer was mistaken, then," I ventured to rejoin, "in telling me that you are a Provençale."

She stared a moment, then she put her nose to her embroidery, which had a dingy, desultory aspect. "Ah, I am a Provençale by birth; but I am a Parisienne by—inclination."

"And by experience, I suppose?" I said.

She questioned me a moment with her hard little eyes. "Oh, experience! I could talk of experience if I wished. I never expected, for example, that experience had *this* in store for me." And she pointed with her bare elbow, and with a jerk of her head, at everything that surrounded her,—at the little white house, the quince-tree, the rickety paling, even at Mr. Mixter.

"You are in exile!" I said, smiling.

"You may imagine what it is! These two years that I have been here I have passed hours—hours! One gets used to things, and sometimes I think I have got used to this. But there are some things that are always beginning over again. For example, my coffee."

"Do you always have coffee at this hour?" I inquired.

She tossed back her head and measured me.

"At what hour would you prefer me to have it? I must have my little cup after breakfast."

"Ah, you breakfast at this hour?"

"At midday—*comme cela se fait*. Here they breakfast at a quarter past seven! That 'quarter past' is charming!"

"But you were telling me about your *coffee?* I observed sympathetically.

"My *cousine* can't believe in it; she can't understand it. She's an excellent girl; but that little cup of black coffee, with a drop of cognac, served at this hour,—they exceed her comprehension. So I have to break the ice every day, and it takes the coffee the time you see to arrive. And when it arrives, monsieur! If I don't offer you any of it you must not take it ill. It will be because I know you have drunk it on the boulevard."

I resented extremely this scornful treatment of poor Caroline Spencer's humble hospitality; but I said nothing, in order to say nothing uncivil. I only looked on Mr. Mixter, who had clasped his arms round his knees and was watching my companion's demonstrative graces in solemn fascination. She presently saw that I was observing him; she glanced at me with a little bold explanatory smile. "You know, he adores me," she murmured, putting her nose into her tapestry again. I expressed the promptest credence, and she went on. "He dreams of becoming my lover! Yes, it's his dream. He has read a French novel; it took him six months. But ever since that he has thought himself the hero, and me the heroine!"

Mr. Mixter had evidently not an idea that he was being talked about; he was too preoccupied with the ecstasy of contemplation. At this moment Caroline Spencer came out of the house, bearing a coffee-pot on a little tray. I noticed that on her way from the door to the table she gave me a single quick, vaguely appealing glance. I wondered what it signified; I felt that it signified a sort of half-frightened longing to know what, as a man of the world who had been in France, I thought of the Countess. It made me extremely uncomfortable. I could not tell her that the Countess was very possibly the runaway wife of a little hair-dresser. I tried suddenly, on the contrary, to show a high consideration for her. But I got up; I could n't stay longer. It vexed me to see Caroline Spencer standing there like a waiting-maid.

"You expect to remain some time at Grimwinter?" I said to the Countess.

She gave a terrible shrug.

"Who knows? Perhaps for years. When one is in misery!—*Chere belle*" she added, turning to Miss Spencer, "you have forgotten the cognac!"

I detained Caroline Spencer as, after looking a moment in silence at the little table, she was turning away to procure this missing delicacy. I silently gave her my hand in farewell. She looked very tired, but there was a strange hint of prospective patience in her severely mild little face. I thought she was rather glad I was going. Mr. Mixter had risen to his feet and was pouring out the Countess's coffee. As I went back past the Baptist church I reflected that poor Miss Spencer had been right in her presentiment that she should still see something of that dear old Europe.

About Author

Henry James OM (15 April 1843 – 28 February 1916) was an American-British author regarded as a key transitional figure between literary realism and literary modernism, and is considered by many to be among the greatest novelists in the English language. He was the son of Henry James Sr. and the brother of renowned philosopher and psychologist William James and diarist Alice James.

He is best known for a number of novels dealing with the social and marital interplay between émigré Americans, English people, and continental Europeans. Examples of such novels include The Portrait of a Lady, The Ambassadors, and The Wings of the Dove. His later works were increasingly experimental. In describing the internal states of mind and social dynamics of his characters, James often made use of a style in which ambiguous or contradictory motives and impressions were overlaid or juxtaposed in the discussion of a character's psyche. For their unique ambiguity, as well as for other aspects of their composition, his late works have been compared to impressionist painting.

His novella The Turn of the Screw has garnered a reputation as the most analysed and ambiguous ghost story in the English language and remains his most widely adapted work in other media. He also wrote a number of other highly regarded ghost stories and is considered one of the greatest masters of the field.

James published articles and books of criticism, travel, biography, autobiography, and plays. Born in the United States, James largely relocated to Europe as a young man and eventually settled in England, becoming a British subject in 1915, one year before his death. James was nominated for the Nobel Prize in Literature in 1911, 1912 and 1916.

Life

Early years, 1843–1883

James was born at 2 Washington Place in New York City on 15 April 1843. His parents were Mary Walsh and Henry James Sr. His father was intelligent and steadfastly congenial. He was a lecturer and philosopher who had inherited independent means from his father, an Albany banker and investor. Mary came from a wealthy family long settled in New York City. Her sister Katherine lived with her adult family for an extended period of time. Henry Jr. had three brothers, William, who was one year his senior, and younger brothers Wilkinson (Wilkie) and Robertson. His younger sister was Alice. Both of his parents were of Irish and Scottish descent.

The family first lived in Albany, at 70 N. Pearl St., and then moved to Fourteenth Street in New York City when James was still a young boy. His education was calculated by his father to expose him to many influences, primarily scientific and philosophical; it was described by Percy Lubbock, the editor of his selected letters, as "extraordinarily haphazard and promiscuous." James did not share the usual education in Latin and Greek classics. Between 1855 and 1860, the James' household traveled to London, Paris, Geneva, Boulogne-sur-Mer and Newport, Rhode Island, according to the father's current interests and publishing ventures, retreating to the United States when funds were low. Henry studied primarily with tutors and briefly attended schools while the family traveled in Europe. Their longest stays were in France, where Henry began to feel at home and became fluent in French. He was afflicted with a stutter, which seems to have manifested itself only when he spoke English; in French, he did not stutter.

In 1860 the family returned to Newport. There Henry became a friend of the painter John La Farge, who introduced him to French literature, and in particular, to Balzac. James later called Balzac his "greatest master," and said that he had learned more about the craft of fiction from him than from anyone else.

In the autumn of 1861 Henry received an injury, probably to his back, while fighting a fire. This injury, which resurfaced at times throughout his life, made him unfit for military service in the American Civil War.

In 1864 the James family moved to Boston, Massachusetts to be near William, who had enrolled first in the Lawrence Scientific School at Harvard and then in the medical school. In 1862 Henry attended Harvard Law School, but realised that he was not interested in studying law. He pursued his interest in literature and associated with authors and critics William Dean Howells and Charles Eliot Norton in Boston and Cambridge, formed lifelong friendships with Oliver Wendell Holmes Jr., the future Supreme Court Justice, and with James and Annie Fields, his first professional mentors.

His first published work was a review of a stage performance, "Miss Maggie Mitchell in Fanchon the Cricket," published in 1863. About a year later, A Tragedy of Error, his first short story, was published anonymously. James's first payment was for an appreciation of Sir Walter Scott's novels, written for the North American Review. He wrote fiction and non-fiction pieces for The Nation and Atlantic Monthly, where Fields was editor. In 1871 he published his first novel, Watch and Ward, in serial form in the Atlantic Monthly. The novel was later published in book form in 1878.

During a 14-month trip through Europe in 1869–70 he met Ruskin, Dickens, Matthew Arnold, William Morris, and George Eliot. Rome impressed him profoundly. "Here I am then in the Eternal City," he wrote to his brother William. "At last—for the first time—I live!" He attempted to support himself as a freelance writer in Rome, then secured a position as Paris correspondent for the New York Tribune, through the influence of its editor John Hay. When these efforts failed he returned to New York City. During 1874 and 1875 he published Transatlantic Sketches, A Passionate Pilgrim, and Roderick Hudson. During this early period in his career he was influenced by Nathaniel Hawthorne.

In 1869 he settled in London. There he established relationships with Macmillan and other publishers, who paid for serial installments that they would later publish in book form. The audience for these serialized novels was largely made up of middle-class women, and James struggled to fashion serious literary work within the strictures imposed by editors' and publishers' notions of what was suitable for young women to read. He lived in rented rooms but was able to join gentlemen's clubs that had libraries and where he could entertain male friends. He was introduced to English society by Henry Adams and Charles Milnes Gaskell, the latter introducing him to the Travellers' and the Reform Clubs.

In the fall of 1875 he moved to the Latin Quarter of Paris. Aside from two trips to America, he spent the next three decades—the rest of his life—in Europe. In Paris he met Zola, Alphonse Daudet, Maupassant, Turgenev, and others. He stayed in Paris only a year before moving to London.

In England he met the leading figures of politics and culture. He continued to be a prolific writer, producing The American (1877), The Europeans (1878), a revision of Watch and Ward (1878), French Poets and Novelists (1878), Hawthorne (1879), and several shorter works of fiction. In 1878 Daisy Miller established his fame on both sides of the Atlantic. It drew notice perhaps mostly because it depicted a woman whose behavior is outside the social norms of Europe. He also began his first masterpiece, The Portrait of a Lady, which would appear in 1881.

In 1877 he first visited Wenlock Abbey in Shropshire, home of his friend Charles Milnes Gaskell whom he had met through Henry Adams. He was much inspired by the darkly romantic Abbey and the surrounding countryside, which features in his essay Abbeys and Castles. In particular the gloomy monastic fishponds behind the Abbey are said to have inspired the lake in The Turn of the Screw.

While living in London, James continued to follow the careers of the "French realists", Émile Zola in particular. Their stylistic methods influenced his own work in the years to come. Hawthorne's influence on him faded during this period, replaced by George Eliot and Ivan Turgenev. 1879–1882 saw the publication of The Europeans, Washington Square, Confidence, and The Portrait of a Lady. He visited America in 1882–1883, then returned to London.

The period from 1881 to 1883 was marked by several losses. His mother died in 1881, followed by his father a few months later, and then by his brother Wilkie. Emerson, an old family friend, died in 1882. His friend Turgenev died in 1883.

Middle years, 1884–1897

In 1884 James made another visit to Paris. There he met again with Zola, Daudet, and Goncourt. He had been following the careers of the French "realist" or "naturalist" writers, and was increasingly influenced by them. In 1886, he published The Bostonians and The Princess Casamassima, both influenced by the French writers he'd studied assiduously. Critical reaction and sales were poor. He wrote to Howells that the books had hurt his career rather than helped because they had "reduced the desire, and demand, for my productions to zero". During this time he became friends with Robert Louis Stevenson, John Singer Sargent, Edmund Gosse, George du Maurier, Paul Bourget, and Constance Fenimore Woolson. His third novel from the 1880s was The Tragic Muse. Although he was following the precepts of Zola in his novels of the '80s, their tone and attitude are closer to the fiction of Alphonse Daudet. The lack of critical and financial success for his novels during this period led him to try writing for the theatre. (His dramatic works and his experiences with theatre are discussed below.)

In the last quarter of 1889, he started translating "for pure and copious lucre" Port Tarascon, the third volume of Alphonse Daudet adventures of Tartarin de Tarascon. Serialized in Harper's Monthly Magazine from June 1890, this translation praised as "clever" by The Spectator was published in January 1891 by Sampson Low, Marston, Searle & Rivington.

After the stage failure of Guy Domville in 1895, James was near despair and thoughts of death plagued him. The years spent on dramatic works were not entirely a loss. As he moved into the last phase of his career he found ways to adapt dramatic techniques into the novel form.

In the late 1880s and throughout the 1890s James made several trips through Europe. He spent a long stay in Italy in 1887. In that year the short novel The Aspern Papers and The Reverberator were published.

Late years, 1898–1916

In 1897–1898 he moved to Rye, Sussex, and wrote The Turn of the Screw. 1899–1900 saw the publication of The Awkward Age and The Sacred

Fount. During 1902–1904 he wrote The Ambassadors, The Wings of the Dove, and The Golden Bowl.

In 1904 he revisited America and lectured on Balzac. In 1906–1910 he published The American Scene and edited the "New York Edition", a 24-volume collection of his works. In 1910 his brother William died; Henry had just joined William from an unsuccessful search for relief in Europe on what then turned out to be his (Henry's) last visit to the United States (from summer 1910 to July 1911), and was near him, according to a letter he wrote, when he died.

In 1913 he wrote his autobiographies, A Small Boy and Others, and Notes of a Son and Brother. After the outbreak of the First World War in 1914 he did war work. In 1915 he became a British subject and was awarded the Order of Merit the following year. He died on 28 February 1916, in Chelsea, London. As he requested, his ashes were buried in Cambridge Cemetery in Massachusetts.

Biographers

James regularly rejected suggestions that he should marry, and after settling in London proclaimed himself "a bachelor". F. W. Dupee, in several volumes on the James family, originated the theory that he had been in love with his cousin Mary ("Minnie") Temple, but that a neurotic fear of sex kept him from admitting such affections: "James's invalidism ... was itself the symptom of some fear of or scruple against sexual love on his part." Dupee used an episode from James's memoir A Small Boy and Others, recounting a dream of a Napoleonic image in the Louvre, to exemplify James's romanticism about Europe, a Napoleonic fantasy into which he fled.

Dupee had not had access to the James family papers and worked principally from James's published memoir of his older brother, William, and the limited collection of letters edited by Percy Lubbock, heavily weighted toward James's last years. His account therefore moved directly from James's childhood, when he trailed after his older brother, to elderly invalidism. As more material became available to scholars, including the diaries of contemporaries and hundreds of affectionate and sometimes erotic letters written by James to younger men, the picture of neurotic celibacy gave way to a portrait of a closeted homosexual.

Between 1953 and 1972, Leon Edel authored a major five-volume biography of James, which accessed unpublished letters and documents after Edel gained the permission of James's family. Edel's portrayal of James included the suggestion he was celibate. It was a view first propounded by critic Saul Rosenzweig in 1943. In 1996 Sheldon M. Novick published Henry James: The Young Master, followed by Henry James: The Mature Master (2007). The first book "caused something of an uproar in Jamesian circles" as it challenged the previous received notion of celibacy, a once-familiar paradigm in biographies of homosexuals when direct evidence was non-existent. Novick also criticised Edel for following the discounted Freudian interpretation of homosexuality "as a kind of failure." The difference of opinion erupted in a series of exchanges between Edel and Novick which were published by the online magazine Slate, with the latter arguing that even the suggestion of celibacy went against James's own injunction "live!"—not "fantasize!"

A letter James wrote in old age to Hugh Walpole has been cited as an explicit statement of this. Walpole confessed to him of indulging in "high jinks", and James wrote a reply endorsing it: "We must know, as much as possible, in our beautiful art, yours & mine, what we are talking about — & the only way to know it is to have lived & loved & cursed & floundered & enjoyed & suffered — I don't think I regret a single 'excess' of my responsive youth".

The interpretation of James as living a less austere emotional life has been subsequently explored by other scholars. The often intense politics of Jamesian scholarship has also been the subject of studies. Author Colm Tóibín has said that Eve Kosofsky Sedgwick's Epistemology of the Closet made a landmark difference to Jamesian scholarship by arguing that he be read as a homosexual writer whose desire to keep his sexuality a secret shaped his layered style and dramatic artistry. According to Tóibín such a reading "removed James from the realm of dead white males who wrote about posh people. He became our contemporary."

James's letters to expatriate American sculptor Hendrik Christian Andersen have attracted particular attention. James met the 27-year-old Andersen in Rome in 1899, when James was 56, and wrote letters to Andersen that are intensely emotional: "I hold you, dearest boy, in my innermost love, & count on your feeling me—in every throb of your soul". In a letter of 6 May 1904, to his brother William, James referred to himself as "always your hopelessly celibate even though sexagenarian Henry". How accurate that description might have been is the subject of contention among James's biographers, but the letters to Andersen were occasionally quasi-erotic: "I put, my dear boy, my arm around you, & feel the pulsation, thereby, as it were, of our excellent future & your admirable endowment." To his homosexual friend Howard Sturgis, James could write: "I repeat, almost to indiscretion, that I could live with you. Meanwhile I can only try to live without you."

His numerous letters to the many young gay men among his close male friends are more forthcoming. In a letter to Howard Sturgis, following a long visit, James refers jocularly to their "happy little congress of two" and in letters to Hugh Walpole he pursues convoluted jokes and puns about their relationship, referring to himself as an elephant who "paws you oh so benevolently" and winds about Walpole his "well meaning old trunk". His letters to Walter Berry printed by the Black Sun Press have long been celebrated for their lightly veiled eroticism.

He corresponded in almost equally extravagant language with his many female friends, writing, for example, to fellow novelist Lucy Clifford: "Dearest Lucy! What shall I say? when I love you so very, very much, and see you nine times for once that I see Others! Therefore I think that—if you want it made clear to the meanest intelligence—I love you more than I love Others." To his New York friend Mary Cadwalader Jones: "Dearest Mary Cadwalader. I yearn over you, but I yearn in vain; & your long silence really breaks my heart, mystifies, depresses, almost alarms me, to the point even of making me wonder if poor unconscious & doting old Célimare [Jones's pet name for James] has 'done' anything, in some dark somnambulism of the spirit, which has ... given you a bad moment, or a wrong impression, or a 'colourable pretext' ... However these things may be, he loves you as tenderly as ever;

nothing, to the end of time, will ever detach him from you, & he remembers those Eleventh St. matutinal intimes hours, those telephonic matinées, as the most romantic of his life ..." His long friendship with American novelist Constance Fenimore Woolson, in whose house he lived for a number of weeks in Italy in 1887, and his shock and grief over her suicide in 1894, are discussed in detail in Edel's biography and play a central role in a study by Lyndall Gordon. (Edel conjectured that Woolson was in love with James and killed herself in part because of his coldness, but Woolson's biographers have objected to Edel's account.)

Works

Style and themes

James is one of the major figures of trans-Atlantic literature. His works frequently juxtapose characters from the Old World (Europe), embodying a feudal civilisation that is beautiful, often corrupt, and alluring, and from the New World (United States), where people are often brash, open, and assertive and embody the virtues—freedom and a more highly evolved moral character—of the new American society. James explores this clash of personalities and cultures, in stories of personal relationships in which power is exercised well or badly. His protagonists were often young American women facing oppression or abuse, and as his secretary Theodora Bosanquet remarked in her monograph Henry James at Work:

> When he walked out of the refuge of his study and into the world and looked around him, he saw a place of torment, where creatures of prey perpetually thrust their claws into the quivering flesh of doomed, defenseless children of light ... His novels are a repeated exposure of this wickedness, a reiterated and passionate plea for the fullest freedom of development, unimperiled by reckless and barbarous stupidity.

Critics have jokingly described three phases in the development of James's prose: "James I, James II, and The Old Pretender." He wrote short stories and plays. Finally, in his third and last period he returned to the long, serialised novel. Beginning in the second period, but most noticeably in the third, he increasingly abandoned direct statement in favour of frequent double negatives, and complex descriptive imagery. Single paragraphs began to run for page after page, in which an initial noun would be succeeded by pronouns surrounded by clouds of adjectives and prepositional clauses, far from their original referents, and verbs would be deferred and then preceded by a series of adverbs. The overall effect could be a vivid evocation of a scene as perceived by a sensitive observer. It has been debated whether this change of style was engendered by James's shifting from writing to dictating to a typist, a change made during the composition of What Maisie Knew.

In its intense focus on the consciousness of his major characters, James's later work foreshadows extensive developments in 20th century fiction. Indeed, he might have influenced stream-of-consciousness writers such as Virginia Woolf, who not only read some of his novels but also wrote essays about them. Both contemporary and modern readers have found the late style difficult and unnecessary; his friend Edith Wharton, who admired him greatly, said that there were passages in his work that were all but incomprehensible. James was harshly portrayed by H. G. Wells as a hippopotamus laboriously attempting to pick up a pea that had got into a corner of its cage. The "late James" style was ably parodied by Max Beerbohm in "The Mote in the Middle Distance".

More important for his work overall may have been his position as an expatriate, and in other ways an outsider, living in Europe. While he came from middle-class and provincial beginnings (seen from the perspective of European polite society) he worked very hard to gain access to all levels of society, and the settings of his fiction range from working class to aristocratic, and often describe the efforts of middle-class Americans to make their way in European capitals. He confessed he got some of his best story ideas from gossip at the dinner table or at country house weekends. He worked for a living, however, and lacked the experiences of select schools, university, and army service, the common bonds of masculine society. He was furthermore a man whose tastes and interests were, according to the prevailing standards of Victorian era Anglo-American culture, rather feminine, and who was shadowed by the cloud of prejudice that then and later accompanied suspicions of his homosexuality. Edmund Wilson famously compared James's objectivity to Shakespeare's:

One would be in a position to appreciate James better if one compared him with the dramatists of the seventeenth century—Racine and Molière, whom he resembles in form as well as in point of view, and even Shakespeare, when allowances are made for the most extreme differences in subject and form. These poets are not, like Dickens and Hardy, writers of melodrama—either humorous or pessimistic, nor secretaries of society like Balzac, nor prophets like Tolstoy: they are occupied simply with the presentation of conflicts of moral character, which they do not concern themselves about softening or averting. They do not indict society for these situations: they regard them as universal and inevitable. They do not even blame God for allowing them: they accept them as the conditions of life.

It is also possible to see many of James's stories as psychological thought-experiments. In his preface to the New York edition of The American he describes the development of the story in his mind as exactly such: the "situation" of an American, "some robust but insidiously beguiled and betrayed, some cruelly wronged, compatriot..." with the focus of the story being on the response of this wronged man. The Portrait of a Lady may be an experiment to see what happens when an idealistic young woman suddenly becomes very rich. In many of his tales, characters seem to exemplify alternative futures and possibilities, as most markedly in "The Jolly Corner", in which the protagonist and a ghost-doppelganger live alternative American and European lives; and in others, like The Ambassadors, an older James seems fondly to regard his own younger self facing a crucial moment.

Major novels

The first period of James's fiction, usually considered to have culminated in The Portrait of a Lady, concentrated on the contrast between Europe and America. The style of these novels is generally straightforward and, though personally characteristic, well within the norms of 19th-century fiction. Roderick Hudson (1875) is a Künstlerroman that traces the development of the title character, an extremely talented sculptor. Although the book shows some signs of immaturity—this was James's first serious attempt at a full-length novel—it has attracted favourable comment due to the vivid realisation of the three major characters: Roderick Hudson, superbly gifted but unstable and unreliable; Rowland Mallet, Roderick's limited but much more mature friend and patron; and Christina Light, one of James's most enchanting and maddening femmes fatales. The pair of Hudson and Mallet has been seen as representing the two sides of James's own nature: the wildly imaginative artist and the brooding conscientious mentor.

In The Portrait of a Lady (1881) James concluded the first phase of his career with a novel that remains his most popular piece of long fiction. The story is of a spirited young American woman, Isabel Archer, who "affronts her destiny" and finds it overwhelming. She inherits a large amount of money and subsequently becomes the victim of Machiavellian scheming by two American expatriates. The narrative is set mainly in Europe, especially in England and Italy. Generally regarded as the masterpiece of his early phase, The Portrait of a Lady is described as a psychological novel, exploring the minds of his characters, and almost a work of social science, exploring the differences between Europeans and Americans, the old and the new worlds.

The second period of James's career, which extends from the publication of The Portrait of a Lady through the end of the nineteenth century, features less popular novels including The Princess Casamassima, published serially in The Atlantic Monthly in 1885–1886, and The Bostonians, published serially in The Century Magazine during the same period. This period also featured James's celebrated Gothic novella, The Turn of the Screw.

The third period of James's career reached its most significant achievement in three novels published just around the start of the 20th century: The Wings of the Dove (1902), The Ambassadors (1903), and The Golden Bowl (1904). Critic F. O. Matthiessen called this "trilogy" James's major phase, and these novels have certainly received intense critical study. It was the second-written of the books, The Wings of the Dove (1902) that was the first published because it attracted no serialization. This novel tells the story of Milly Theale, an American heiress stricken with a serious disease, and her impact on the people around her. Some of these people befriend Milly with honourable motives, while others are more self-interested. James stated in his autobiographical books that Milly was based on Minny Temple, his beloved cousin who died at an early age of tuberculosis. He said that he attempted in the novel to wrap her memory in the "beauty and dignity of art".

Shorter narratives

James was particularly interested in what he called the "beautiful and blest nouvelle", or the longer form of short narrative. Still, he produced a number of very short stories in which he achieved notable compression of sometimes complex subjects. The following narratives are representative of James's achievement in the shorter forms of fiction.

- "A Tragedy of Error" (1864), short story
- "The Story of a Year" (1865), short story
- A Passionate Pilgrim (1871), novella
- Madame de Mauves (1874), novella
- Daisy Miller (1878), novella
- The Aspern Papers (1888), novella
- The Lesson of the Master (1888), novella
- The Pupil (1891), short story
- "The Figure in the Carpet" (1896), short story
- The Beast in the Jungle (1903), novella
- An International Episode (1878)
- Picture and Text
- Four Meetings (1885)
- A London Life, and Other Tales (1889)
- The Spoils of Poynton (1896)

- Embarrassments (1896)
- The Two Magics: The Turn of the Screw, Covering End (1898)
- A Little Tour of France (1900)
- The Sacred Fount (1901)
- Views and Reviews (1908)
- The Wings of the Dove, Volume I (1902)
- The Wings of the Dove, Volume II (1909)
- The Finer Grain (1910)
- The Outcry (1911)
- Lady Barbarina: The Siege of London, An International Episode and Other Tales (1922)
- The Birthplace (1922)

Plays

At several points in his career James wrote plays, beginning with one-act plays written for periodicals in 1869 and 1871 and a dramatisation of his popular novella Daisy Miller in 1882. From 1890 to 1892, having received a bequest that freed him from magazine publication, he made a strenuous effort to succeed on the London stage, writing a half-dozen plays of which only one, a dramatisation of his novel The American, was produced. This play was performed for several years by a touring repertory company and had a respectable run in London, but did not earn very much money for James. His other plays written at this time were not produced.

In 1893, however, he responded to a request from actor-manager George Alexander for a serious play for the opening of his renovated St. James's Theatre, and wrote a long drama, Guy Domville, which Alexander produced. There was a noisy uproar on the opening night, 5 January 1895, with hissing from the gallery when James took his bow after the final curtain, and the author was upset. The play received moderately good reviews and had a modest run of four weeks before being taken off to make way for Oscar Wilde's The Importance of Being Earnest, which Alexander thought would have better prospects for the coming season.

After the stresses and disappointment of these efforts James insisted that he would write no more for the theatre, but within weeks had agreed to write a curtain-raiser for Ellen Terry. This became the one-act "Summersoft", which he later rewrote into a short story, "Covering End", and then expanded into a full-length play, The High Bid, which had a brief run in London in 1907, when James made another concerted effort to write for the stage. He wrote three new plays, two of which were in production when the death of Edward VII on 6 May 1910 plunged London into mourning and theatres closed. Discouraged by failing health and the stresses of theatrical work, James did not renew his efforts in the theatre, but recycled his plays as successful novels. The Outcry was a best-seller in the United States when it was published in 1911. During the years 1890–1893 when he was most engaged with the theatre, James wrote a good deal of theatrical criticism and assisted Elizabeth Robins and others in translating and producing Henrik Ibsen for the first time in London.

Leon Edel argued in his psychoanalytic biography that James was traumatised by the opening night uproar that greeted Guy Domville, and that it plunged him into a prolonged depression. The successful later novels, in Edel's view, were the result of a kind of self-analysis, expressed in fiction, which partly freed him from his fears. Other biographers and scholars have not accepted this account, however; the more common view being that of F.O. Matthiessen, who wrote: "Instead of being crushed by the collapse of his hopes [for the theatre]... he felt a resurgence of new energy."

Non-fiction

Beyond his fiction, James was one of the more important literary critics in the history of the novel. In his classic essay The Art of Fiction (1884), he argued against rigid prescriptions on the novelist's choice of subject and method of treatment. He maintained that the widest possible freedom in content and approach would help ensure narrative fiction's continued vitality.

James wrote many valuable critical articles on other novelists; typical is his book-length study of Nathaniel Hawthorne, which has been the subject of critical debate. Richard Brodhead has suggested that the study was emblematic of James's struggle with Hawthorne's influence, and constituted an effort to place the elder writer "at a disadvantage." Gordon Fraser, meanwhile, has suggested that the study was part of a more commercial effort by James to introduce himself to British readers as Hawthorne's natural successor.

When James assembled the New York Edition of his fiction in his final years, he wrote a series of prefaces that subjected his own work to searching, occasionally harsh criticism.

At 22 James wrote The Noble School of Fiction for The Nation's first issue in 1865. He would write, in all, over 200 essays and book, art, and theatre reviews for the magazine.

For most of his life James harboured ambitions for success as a playwright. He converted his novel The American into a play that enjoyed modest returns in the early 1890s. In all he wrote about a dozen plays, most of which went unproduced. His costume drama Guy Domville failed disastrously on its opening night in 1895. James then largely abandoned his efforts to conquer the stage and returned to his fiction. In his Notebooks he maintained that his theatrical experiment benefited his novels and tales by helping him dramatise his characters' thoughts and emotions. James produced a small but valuable amount of theatrical criticism, including perceptive appreciations of Henrik Ibsen.

With his wide-ranging artistic interests, James occasionally wrote on the visual arts. Perhaps his most valuable contribution was his favourable assessment of fellow expatriate John Singer Sargent, a painter whose critical status has improved markedly in recent decades. James also wrote sometimes charming, sometimes brooding articles about various places he visited and lived in. His most famous books of travel writing include Italian Hours (an example of the charming approach) and The American Scene (most definitely on the brooding side).

James was one of the great letter-writers of any era. More than ten thousand of his personal letters are extant, and over three thousand have been published in a large number of collections. A complete edition of James's letters began publication in 2006, edited by Pierre Walker and Greg Zacharias. As of 2014, eight volumes have been published, covering the period from 1855 to 1880. James's correspondents included celebrated contemporaries like Robert Louis Stevenson, Edith Wharton and Joseph Conrad, along with many others in his wide circle of friends and acquaintances. The letters range from the "mere twaddle of graciousness" to serious discussions of artistic, social and personal issues.

Very late in life James began a series of autobiographical works: A Small Boy and Others, Notes of a Son and Brother, and the unfinished The Middle Years. These books portray the development of a classic observer who was passionately interested in artistic creation but was somewhat reticent about participating fully in the life around him.

Reception

Criticism, biographies and fictional treatments

James's work has remained steadily popular with the limited audience of educated readers to whom he spoke during his lifetime, and has remained firmly in the canon, but, after his death, some American critics, such as Van Wyck Brooks, expressed hostility towards James for his long expatriation and eventual naturalisation as a British subject. Other critics such as E. M. Forster complained about what they saw as James's squeamishness in the treatment of sex and other possibly controversial material, or dismissed his late style as difficult and obscure, relying heavily on extremely long sentences and excessively latinate language. Similarly Oscar Wilde criticised him for writing "fiction as if it were a painful duty". Vernon Parrington, composing a canon of American literature, condemned James for having cut himself off from America. Jorge Luis Borges wrote about him, "Despite the scruples and delicate complexities of James, his work suffers from a major defect: the absence of life." And Virginia Woolf, writing to Lytton Strachey, asked, "Please tell me what you find in Henry James. ... we have his works here, and

I read, and I can't find anything but faintly tinged rose water, urbane and sleek, but vulgar and pale as Walter Lamb. Is there really any sense in it?" The novelist W. Somerset Maugham wrote, "He did not know the English as an Englishman instinctively knows them and so his English characters never to my mind quite ring true," and argued "The great novelists, even in seclusion, have lived life passionately. Henry James was content to observe it from a window." Maugham nevertheless wrote, "The fact remains that those last novels of his, notwithstanding their unreality, make all other novels, except the very best, unreadable." Colm Tóibín observed that James "never really wrote about the English very well. His English characters don't work for me."

Despite these criticisms, James is now valued for his psychological and moral realism, his masterful creation of character, his low-key but playful humour, and his assured command of the language. In his 1983 book, The Novels of Henry James, Edward Wagenknecht offers an assessment that echoes Theodora Bosanquet's:

> "To be completely great," Henry James wrote in an early review, "a work of art must lift up the heart," and his own novels do this to an outstanding degree ... More than sixty years after his death, the great novelist who sometimes professed to have no opinions stands foursquare in the great Christian humanistic and democratic tradition. The men and women who, at the height of World War II, raided the secondhand shops for his out-of-print books knew what they were about. For no writer ever raised a braver banner to which all who love freedom might adhere.

William Dean Howells saw James as a representative of a new realist school of literary art which broke with the English romantic tradition epitomised by the works of Charles Dickens and William Makepeace Thackeray. Howells wrote that realism found "its chief exemplar in Mr. James... A novelist he is not, after the old fashion, or after any fashion but his own." F.R. Leavis championed Henry James as a novelist of "established pre-eminence" in The Great Tradition (1948), asserting that The Portrait of a Lady and The Bostonians were "the two most brilliant novels in the language." James is now prized as a master of point of view who moved literary fiction forward by insisting in showing, not telling, his stories to the reader. (Source: Wikipedia)

NOTABLE WORKS

NOVELS

Watch and Ward (1871)

Roderick Hudson (1875)

The American (1877)

The Europeans (1878)

Confidence (1879)

Washington Square (1880)

The Portrait of a Lady (1881)

The Bostonians (1886)

The Princess Casamassima (1886)

The Reverberator (1888)

The Tragic Muse (1890)

The Other House (1896)

The Spoils of Poynton (1897)

What Maisie Knew (1897)

The Awkward Age (1899)

The Sacred Fount (1901)

The Wings of the Dove (1902)

The Ambassadors (1903)

The Golden Bowl (1904)

The Whole Family (collaborative novel with eleven other authors, 1908)

The Outcry (1911)

The Ivory Tower (unfinished, published posthumously 1917)

The Sense of the Past (unfinished, published posthumously 1917)

SHORT STORIES AND NOVELLAS

A Tragedy of Error (1864)

The Story of a Year (1865)

A Landscape Painter (1866)

A Day of Days (1866)

My Friend Bingham (1867)

Poor Richard (1867)

The Story of a Masterpiece (1868)

A Most Extraordinary Case (1868)

A Problem (1868)

De Grey: A Romance (1868)

Osborne's Revenge (1868)

The Romance of Certain Old Clothes (1868)

A Light Man (1869)

Gabrielle de Bergerac (1869)

Travelling Companions (1870)

A Passionate Pilgrim (1871)

At Isella (1871)

Master Eustace (1871)

Guest's Confession (1872)

The Madonna of the Future (1873)

The Sweetheart of M. Briseux (1873)

The Last of the Valerii (1874)

Madame de Mauves (1874)

Adina (1874)

Professor Fargo (1874)

Eugene Pickering (1874)

Benvolio (1875)

Crawford's Consistency (1876)

The Ghostly Rental (1876)

Four Meetings (1877)

Rose-Agathe (1878, as Théodolinde)

Daisy Miller (1878)

Longstaff's Marriage (1878)

An International Episode (1878)

The Pension Beaurepas (1879)

A Diary of a Man of Fifty (1879)

A Bundle of Letters (1879)

The Point of View (1882)

The Siege of London (1883)

Impressions of a Cousin (1883)

Lady Barberina (1884)

Pandora (1884)

The Author of Beltraffio (1884)

Georgina's Reasons (1884)

A New England Winter (1884)

The Path of Duty (1884)

Mrs. Temperly (1887)

Louisa Pallant (1888)

The Aspern Papers (1888)

The Liar (1888)

The Modern Warning (1888, originally published as The Two Countries)

A London Life (1888)

The Patagonia (1888)

The Lesson of the Master (1888)

The Solution (1888)

The Pupil (1891)

Brooksmith (1891)

The Marriages (1891)

The Chaperon (1891)

Sir Edmund Orme (1891)

Nona Vincent (1892)

The Real Thing (1892)

The Private Life (1892)

Lord Beaupré (1892)

The Visits (1892)

Sir Dominick Ferrand (1892)

Greville Fane (1892)

Collaboration (1892)

Owen Wingrave (1892)

The Wheel of Time (1892)

The Middle Years (1893)

The Death of the Lion (1894)

The Coxon Fund (1894)

The Next Time (1895)

Glasses (1896)

The Altar of the Dead (1895)

The Figure in the Carpet (1896)

The Way It Came (1896, also published as The Friends of the Friends)

The Turn of the Screw (1898)

Covering End (1898)

In the Cage (1898)

John Delavoy (1898)

The Given Case (1898)

Europe (1899)

The Great Condition (1899)

The Real Right Thing (1899)

Paste (1899)

The Great Good Place (1900)

Maud-Evelyn (1900)

Miss Gunton of Poughkeepsie (1900)

The Tree of Knowledge (1900)

The Abasement of the Northmores (1900)

The Third Person (1900)

The Special Type (1900)

The Tone of Time (1900)

Broken Wings (1900)

The Two Faces (1900)

Mrs. Medwin (1901)

The Beldonald Holbein (1901)

The Story in It (1902)

Flickerbridge (1902)

The Birthplace (1903)

The Beast in the Jungle (1903)

The Papers (1903)

Fordham Castle (1904)

Julia Bride (1908)

The Jolly Corner (1908)

The Velvet Glove (1909)

Mora Montravers (1909)

Crapy Cornelia (1909)

The Bench of Desolation (1909)

A Round of Visits (1910)

OTHER

Transatlantic Sketches (1875)

French Poets and Novelists (1878)

Hawthorne (1879)

Portraits of Places (1883)

A Little Tour in France (1884)

Partial Portraits (1888)

Essays in London and Elsewhere (1893)

Picture and Text (1893)

Terminations (1893)

Theatricals (1894)

Theatricals: Second Series (1895)

Guy Domville (1895)

The Soft Side (1900)

William Wetmore Story and His Friends (1903)

The Better Sort (1903)

English Hours (1905)

The Question of our Speech; The Lesson of Balzac. Two Lectures (1905)

The American Scene (1907)

Views and Reviews (1908)

Italian Hours (1909)

A Small Boy and Others (1913)

Notes on Novelists (1914)

Notes of a Son and Brother (1914)

Within the Rim (1918)

Travelling Companions (1919)

Notebooks (various, published posthumously)

The Middle Years (unfinished, published posthumously 1917)

A Most Unholy Trade (1925, published posthumously)

The Art of the Novel : Critical Prefaces (1934)

CPSIA information can be obtained
at www.ICGtesting.com
Printed in the USA
LVHW052046021120
670493LV00002B/6

9 781662 714153